Companion Pieces

A Novel

by

H. Reese

Cover Photo: Lisa Rosenberg
Production: Foglia Publications
Editing Assistance: Mae Kaven, The Last Detail
Printing: DeHarts Media Services

ISBN: 0-615-12860-2

To Order:
Companion Press
PO Box 23006,
San Jose, CA 95153-3006
companionpress@juno.com

Group orders over 5 copies, take off 10%.
Price per copy is $14.95. Add $2.00 for postage and handling.

We dedicate this work to Emma Eljas
with our love.
We would never have finished this novel
if it hadn't been for you.

Acknowledgments

For their inspired assistance with this project, we sincerely thank our computer wizard, Paul Gendler, who taught the machine to behave; Valerie Wagner, who helped us get past a massive writers' block; and Lisa Rosenberg, poet turned photographer on our behalf — just in time.

*When people get together and work well over time,
the fabric of their lives forms a patchwork
that we call Companion Pieces.*

One

Listen lady, your husband is in bed with another woman and he is making twice the money you think he is. Listen lady, your husband is... The woman's steely voice echoed in Allison's memory. She could hear the cruel assessment and feel herself cringe under her cold, direct stare. She remembered recoiling from the shocking words that she felt could not possibly be true.

Allison hadn't expected to meet Felice Montgomery again after all these years. Was it fifteen? And here of all places, when Allison was the featured speaker at the luncheon of the San Francisco Bay Area Council for Children, was not the best time. Nonetheless, she and Felice had just made eye contact through the crowd of well-dressed women. Allison was startled. Her half-smile reflected the multitude of feelings that rushed through her—surprise, embarrassment at remembering the tumultuous times they had shared, and gratitude for what Felice had accomplished on her behalf.

This unexpected link to her past engulfed Allison with a flood of memories, especially of the afternoon she had first gone to Felice's office. It was a month after Alex had walked out of their marriage. In those dreary February days, Allison had run out of funds and had been forced to borrow a couple of dollars from her next-door neighbor to take the kids to McDonald's. She had to offer the neighbor some reason for her dilemma, so she related a few details about Alex having moved out. As she stood by the open door, her neighbor's husband looked up from his newspaper. "What you really need is a good divorce lawyer," he said.

Allison blanched. "But I don't want a divorce. Besides, all the attorneys I know are Alex's friends, and I don't even have the price of a babysitter."

"Don't worry," the fellow said, "my wife will watch the kids, won't you, honey? And Felice Montgomery would be a terrific lawyer for you."

Allison's brain wasn't working yet. In fact, she wondered if she would ever be able to think on her own again. She didn't know what else to do, so she thanked the neighbors for the money and the phone number they put into her hand and went back to the wide-eyed children waiting in the car. After a few more days with no word from Alex, Allison knew that she would need help in order to get any money from him. She retrieved the crumpled piece of paper with the phone number on it from the bottom of her purse.

She had felt relieved when the neighbor recommended a female attorney. *That's just what I could use now,* Allison remembered thinking. *Someone to put her arms around me, be sympathetic, let me shed some tears on her shoulder. If this woman is a divorce attorney, she must know that I'm feeling as if I have a bloody stump where my marriage has just been amputated. She'll understand the pain in my heart. Perhaps she and I can even become friends.*

Allison couldn't have been more wrong. Felice had a large

office overlooking the Embarcadero in San Francisco. Lots of cold glass windows, and no warmth in the office decor nor in the woman who presided over it. Felice had remained seated, elbows folded on her desk as Allison began to pour out the litany of Alex's sudden leaving. Only a few sentences into the story, she had been cut short by Felice, who uttered the statement that now reverberated in Allison's bones. "Listen, lady, your husband is in bed with another woman, and he's making twice the money you think he is."

Allison had stared blankly at this hateful woman. What she needed now was some understanding, not lies. But how could this stranger know that Alex always told her everything, that Alex was so honest and so fair and so...? Allison could see from her expression that Felice was listening to her denials as skeptically as she had probably listened to the pleas of many other suddenly-abandoned wives. Finally, Felice picked up a pen and filled in a few words and numbers on a legal form and pushed it across the desk toward Allison.

Felice said quietly, but firmly, "I want you to sign this *Application For Order To Show Cause.*"

Allison glanced at the amounts Felice had written for spousal and child support and immediately objected. "Don't be ridiculous! He doesn't even make that much money in total, and *he* needs to live, too."

"If you're going to believe the lies he has fed you all these years, then please don't waste my time," was the icy reply.

Allison was weary. She didn't know any other attorneys, and she didn't have anyone else to watch the children even if she could change attorneys. She reached for the form.

Signing that paper turned out to be one of the best things she had ever done in her life.

Felice and Allison met in the glass office throughout the long divorce process, but they never became friends. Instead, Allison continued to fight her whenever possible, as it was easier to make Felice the enemy than Alex. She found herself protesting and defending an Alex who no longer existed, if indeed the person she thought she knew had ever existed. Felice refused to be thrown off stride, however. As an experienced attorney, she knew that men don't often leave one nest until they have another one feathered. An accountant who was planning to leave his wife would automatically have started hiding assets long before his departure.

At the end, Allison had intended to admit to Felice that her professional judgment about Alex had been correct all along, but the time never seemed right. Through financial haggling with Alex's attorney, Felice had succeeded in getting Allison and the children more than enough money. But the settlement didn't bring any joy to Allison. By the time she got it, she knew for certain that Alex was happily ensconced in Berkeley with his new hippie girlfriend.

———◦◦◦———

Felice turned her gaze away from the other businesswomen at her table and looked around the banquet room. *Don't tell me my mother has backed out again.* Then her glance fell on an attractive redhead, the center of attention in a cluster of people near the front. The woman looked familiar. Felice was sure she knew her; she put her brain in search mode and concentrated. *Allison Evans. That's who it is. Allison Evans.*

She remembered the scared look in Allison's eyes when she had first come to her office. The husband had pulled a "sudden notice act," leaving her with three kids and no money. Felice had been sure she would be able to locate assets that Allison didn't know about. She smiled, thinking about the damned good settlement she had gotten for her. She knew that women like Allison might find her a little tough, but she had seen to it that those three kids were taken care of, and Allison, too, until she got on her feet.

Allison looked more attractive now. Her auburn hair was cut short, in stylish curls, and she evidently had learned to use a bit of makeup to accentuate her hazel eyes. *She must be wearing very high heels,* Felice thought. Allison looked taller than Felice remembered. Or maybe it was just that she stood more erect.

Allison glanced up and stared at Felice for a few seconds. *She recognizes me.* Felice turned away and vainly looked around again for her mother. Skimming over the program, Felice saw that the talk would be given by someone named Allison Boyce. Was it possible that her timid former client could be Allison Boyce, today's featured speaker?

⚍◈⚍

Carol parked in a public lot and walked to the Carlton Hotel. She paused briefly in front of a bookstore window to look over the display of best-sellers. For a moment she slipped her aching left foot out of the navy pump. It had been a while since she'd worn heels, and that darn bunion was bothering her again. Carol liked to see what was newly published and she always checked whether the author's name on the cover was larger than the title of the book. She knew that meant the author had "arrived," and it was likely her trendy book group would soon be reading something by that person.

In the lobby of the hotel where the luncheon was being held, the stay-at-homes like Carol, in their spring print and pastel dresses, stood together in twos and threes. Carol was wearing her new robin-egg blue dress and jacket set. Working women like her daughter were in their "power suits," as Felice called them. Carol stood apart, the odd one out, but she didn't mind. She was determined since her husband's death three years ago that she would lead her own life, uninfluenced by social demands or her daughter.

She still lived in the large home she and Robert had purchased, with all its memories of the entertaining they had done for his business friends. More and more frequently, she was considering moving to smaller quarters—a new condo perhaps. At sixty years, she had earned her independence. Carol tried to spot Felice, who had a morning appearance in Superior Court for a child custody case. Felice had said if she got out early enough she'd come over to the hotel for the luncheon. Carol wondered if there would be anyone she knew to sit with, in case Felice didn't show.

Carol scanned the room again. She figured Felice would be wearing a large hat, and that was what she looked for. *Too many women in hats these days. I'll never find her.* At a table off to the right Carol thought she saw the petite French woman she'd met last year at the widow's group. Yes, it was Monique. Carol waved. Monique rushed over and gave her a kiss on each cheek.

"I'm so glad to see someone I know," Carol confessed. "I

haven't seen you since that dance we went to together a month or two ago. Is there...?" She glanced over to where Monique had been sitting. "Is there room for one more at your table?"

"Oh, I'm so sorry," Monique answered. "Every seat is occupied. If I had known you were coming, I'd have saved you a place." She squeezed Carol's hand. "But how about us getting together next week for a walk and a talk?"

"Sounds good," Carol replied. "I'll call you."

Carol still could not find her daughter, so she sat down at a table where there were several empty chairs. The women there stopped talking and introduced themselves, but returned to their conversation. Under the table, Carol slipped off her pumps.

⟫⟩◈⟨⟪

To Maevis, the banquet room was a mosaic of bobbing heads with hair styled to perfection, a sea of wave and weave of every hue. *Not another free-flowing, natural-colored mane like mine in the bunch,* she decided, peering in from the doorway. *Okay, So I am somewhat smug about my tresses,* she conceded to herself. *But a girl's gotta recognize her own good points, doesn't she?*

Maevis waylaid a woman with a name tag and asked the whereabouts of the person in charge. "Right over there, see those two talking?" The woman answered, pointing. "The fair-haired shorter one is Josephine Chapelle, our president. You might recognize her from TV. She does news reporting."

"Thanks so much," Maevis called to the air behind her as she strode towards the two women and extended her arm between them. "Hello there, Josephine, or should I call you Madame Chairwoman?" Maevis shook hands with the surprised blonde. "I'm Maevis with an 'e' and I'm a first-timer here today. My friend Annie — you must know her, Annie Ross — was supposed to be here today, but I guess she flaked out. Probably got immersed in mopping the kitchen floor or something. Anyway, she's a member of your organization and she told me all about the work you do to help kids. I think it's wonderful. I have children myself and I hope to participate in your projects when I get time. Maybe in about ten years!" She laughed. "Well, nice meeting you and don't worry about me. I'll find myself a seat." Maevis glided away.

"Now, where were we?" Josephine winked at Allison, who was frowning as she watched Maevis depart.

Making her way across the room, Maevis chose Table 6. *My lucky number. That's the spot I shall grace with my presence.* She pulled out a vacant chair next to a silver-haired woman who looked old enough to be her mother, but was far more stylish. Maevis noticed that her light blue suit jacket was impeccably tailored. Her bright white hair was short and she had lovely pearls around her neck. The suit, Maevis saw, matched the woman's eyes.

"Is this seat available?" Maevis asked, and without waiting for an answer she reached for a water goblet and downed its contents in a few gulps.

Carol looked at the younger woman. Long turquoise stones dangled from her earlobes. A flowered skirt reached to her ankles and bare toes stuck out from leather sandals.

"Why yes, it is available. Do sit down, please." Carol patted the chair. "I've been waiting for you."

"Really?" Maevis squinted at Carol, then guffawed loudly. "Oh, you're teasing. And you got me, you did! I'm so darned gullible." She put out her hand, a ring on every finger. "Maevis with an *e* here, and you are...?"

"Carol Montgomery. It's nice to meet you. That's an interesting name," Carol said. "Withanee. I don't think I've heard that one before."

"Withanee?" Maevis poked at her loose, dark hair. "Oh, no," she laughed again. "That's not my last name. I said 'I'm Maevis with an *e*,' see, because it's usually spelled M-a-v-i-s, but I'm named after Granny Maeve so my parents left in the *e* — M-a-e-v-i-s."

She swung off her fringed shoulder bag and sat down, still talking.

"This is my first time here, and I hate to come to these things alone, don't you? But how else are you going to meet people? I've heard a lot about the work this group does for kids — it's so vital, don't you think?"

Carol had been glancing around the room again for a sign of her daughter, but to no avail. She decided to forget about finding Felice and turned back to the young woman next to her. She had a sense this was going to be an interesting afternoon.

"Yes, I do think it's important," she answered Maevis, "I'm a new member myself. The program says that today's speaker will be talking about saving a child during the war. I work as a volunteer at a home for abused women and their youngsters, so I'm eager to hear what she has to say."

"Oh, you're a volunteer? That's fantastic. I also believe in helping children — mostly my own. I have three. I think children are the future of our society. Don't you just hate to see those little lost faces on the grocery bags? And I worry about the poor moms who have foul-tempered husbands. We all have to do what we can to help, don't you think?"

"I certainly do. My daughter is an attorney who specializes in domestic law. She's been active in the Bay Area Council for Children for many years and finally got me to join. I think I keep busy enough, but Felice thinks I need to increase my social activities."

"Really? Why?" Maevis reached past Carol to the pitcher, refilling her glass. "Excuse me, but I need more H_2O." She drank and put down the empty glass. "Surely you don't sit at home and knit all day, when you're not volunteering, do you, Carol? Not that there's anything wrong with knitting, of course. If I'm not being too nosy, that is," Maevis added.

"Not at all," Carol said. "Since my husband passed away I've been living alone. My daughter is always prodding me to be with people more. She won't accept that I enjoy being by myself at times."

"I understand perfectly," Maevis replied. "I, for instance, charge around all day driving my kids here and there, running errands and "interfacing," as my husband calls it. Believe it or not, I fantasize about lying on a quiet beach somewhere — all alone."

Carol smiled and her eyes lit up. "When my Robert was alive, not only was I raising our daughter, but I went with him to all his business functions, so I know what it means to be constantly on the go. There were frequent conventions, luncheons for prospective clients and even some reward trips for being the best in his firm. He was a top stockbroker and I was always busy hostessing, entertaining for him. Now, I like doing what *I* want to do."

"Go girl, go!" Maevis reached again for the water pitcher. "Sorry, but I'm parched. Neal and I were trying to keep the romance alive last night. We had champagne and caviar in bed, that's why I'm so thirsty —" Maevis stopped. "Oh, there I go again. Always putting my foot in my mouth. I apologize, Carol. You just told me that your husband's gone and here I am blabbing about Neal and bed and all my favorite things."

"Don't be ridiculous." Carol put her hand over Maevis' and gave it a pat. "Sure I miss my husband, but I'm doing just fine on my own. As I said, I actually *like* being by myself, even though I can't seem to convince Felice of that."

"And which one is she, your daughter?" Maevis asked.

Carol turned and scanned the room. "There she is," she pointed. "The one in the red hat, near the front of the room." Carol sighed. "I thought she was going to sit with me, but I guess she found some colleagues. Felice is a real workaholic, constantly networking."

Maevis flipped her hair off her neck. "Well, I couldn't stand to wear heels and a suit everyday," she commented. "Clothes like that are too confining for my taste. Those career women can have their business lunches. I'd feel too repressed." Maevis wiggled her toes inside her sandals. "Though I do love hats," she added, smiling at Carol.

Carol returned the smile. "We'll talk more later," she whispered, as they both looked toward the podium, where Josephine was tapping a gavel.

———➤◆⊲———

Allison had been reluctant to read her Jonas story at the luncheon, but Josephine was persuasive. So Allison had arranged for a substitute teacher to take over her class at Union Elementary School. Lately, she had been feeling a little blue and hoped she could elevate her mood by buying a new outfit and doing a terrific job as speaker. One afternoon after school, she'd combed the stores and had found a beautiful moss-green silk dress with a swirling skirt that showed off her small waist, made her feel almost ten years younger, and was perfect with her auburn hair. Now, standing at the head table next to Josephine, Allison leaned close and whispered. "Jo, I didn't expect this kind of a turnout, did you?"

"Never a doubt, sweetie."

"But Jo, I just saw my old attorney. The one from the divorce. I don't know if I can get through this."

"Allison, anybody who can handle thirty second-graders like you can has nothing to worry about. You'll be fine." Josephine put her arm around Allison and gave her a warm squeeze. Then Josephine moved to the dais and surveyed the crowd. Things were going well. She'd chosen a good committee, chaired by efficient Monique, and together they had delegated responsibilities while still keeping an eye on all the details. She felt pleased with herself as she started the introduction.

"The world today is often indifferent to our needs," Allison heard Jo saying. "There is cruelty everywhere we look. We are horrified at the stories we read. The violence chills our hearts and makes us grieve. But this is not the entire story." Josephine paused. "In keeping with the goals of the Bay Area Council for Children, today's theme is about a person who did more than just help a child. Our speaker has a tale to tell of kindness at great personal sacrifice during the terrible days of World War II. We will be hearing from my dear friend, Allison Boyce. Allison is a dedicated elementary school teacher, a mother to five and a woman with a continuing interest in children in trouble. This interest grew out of a chance meeting with Jonas, who had been one of many thousands of children hidden during the Second World War. Today, Allison will share Jonas' story with us.

"Hidden children during World War II?" Maevis asked Carol in a loud whisper.

"That's how they saved some of the Jewish youngsters," Carol said quietly.

"But I thought..."

"Shhhh." Carol turned her attention to the speaker.

Allison was adjusting the microphone. She glanced around the room at the staring faces. She was surprised to see one very familiar figure. *Was that Brad at the back? He hadn't said anything about coming.* She might be mistaken. Allison blocked out all the distractions and went on automatic. She could only hope her story would satisfy the expectations of her audience.

"Thank you, Josephine, for that lovely introduction." Allison took a deep breath. "About seven years ago, I was on my honeymoon in Europe with my second husband when we met a Dutch couple at a concert. They spoke English quite well and were eager to converse with Americans. An after-concert drink was followed by more invitations. One Sunday the man, whose name was Jonas, suggested we join him and his wife for a ride in the country." Allison paused and took another look toward the back of the room. *Yes, it was Brad.*

"Jonas was a little vague about where we were going, but eventually he divulged that we were about to visit the people who had saved him, a Jewish boy of nine, during the Nazi occupation. Of course, we had heard of these happenings during the war, but for an American with no personal wartime experiences, to meet and speak with a real live hero was moving beyond words.

"In the tiny front room of the farmhouse, Jonas revealed to us how it came to be that Olef, a Dutch farmer, risked his own life to save that of one young Jewish boy, and I was so taken with their experience that I felt the need to write it down. The piece I am about to read to you is that story. I hope you enjoy it.

The simple-faced man loomed large over the small boy whose hand he was holding. The man's eyes were anxious, his bearing upright. Seven minutes after one o'clock. Perhaps the traffic, he said to himself with a slight encouraging nod to the boy. Nine minutes after one.

The black hands of the station's grand clock moved yet another minute. We must not look suspicious. The SS... He grasped the boy's hand more tightly. Uncertain, he walked to the nearest window, eyes searching for someone who might be from the underground. No one. No one at all.

Everyone else appeared to be hurrying someplace or other, eyes lowered, half fearful themselves of being stopped by one of the uniforms. And here he was, amidst the busy crowd, standing humbly, idly, with a small boy, like a stupid lost sheep and its lamb. And like the sheep we will be led to slaughter if I, Olef, do not do something now.

Dummkopf, what is to do? Do I know where the under-ground hides Jews? Do I know what to do with a nine year old boy? Or is it possible, can I, should I just walk away from him as if nothing had happened?

He is small for his age. He is staring at me. He knows, he knows we are in trouble. God, he and his kind have been in trouble here in Europe since long before he was born. He knows that I wish I hadn't promised his father. He knows I am about to go out those big doors by myself.

Come, Jonas, we must go now. *He looks at me, his eyes full of unspoken questions. I have no answer yet; I have only his hand holding mine. Why don't they come, these people whose job it is to hide the Jews? I'm only from the country. I do not know what the underground does. But you daren't leave a small Jew-boy alone at the train station, not in these terrible times.*

Jonas, come. You and I, we will get some coffee in a shop nearby. It will be all right. *How will I make it all right? Where will I hide this boy from the danger that is everywhere?*

Do fathers take their sons for coffee? I never had a son. I am too old to be this boy's father. He is dressed too finely to be a farmer's son. Dear Lord, let no one notice. Dear God, fill my big empty head with a plan.

Jonas, eat your roll, drink the coffee. We are going to take a ride to my farm. We will have a good time, a little holiday. My wagon is just nearby. *The boy is silent. His hand feels small. He is frightened, but does not tremble.*

Jonas, there is a little park across the street. I want you to run and play while I get the wagon. In the park you must put some dirt on your clothes. You must leave your shoes hidden between the bushes. For a little while you must try to look like the son of Olef, the farmer.

His eyes say no, but he walks toward the park with resolve. He is intelligent. He knows it is our only chance. He looks back at me as if to wish me with his eyes that I return quickly... that I come back, come back for him.

What am I doing? What will Helga say? What if we are questioned? Poor Helga. Her big, stupid husband shot for holding the hand of a small boy. I could drive the other way. I must think of Helga. I am all she has.

What would Helga do? Always she helps me care for the littlest lamb, the piglet runt. If we save God's helpless animals, how can we forget this small human creature? They are rounding up more of the Jews every day. Any minute Jonas' family will be taken, taken someplace.

The last time Mr. Knopp and I went fishing together, we spoke. We had fished together many times before, when he took his holiday in our village. But this time he did not come for the fish. He came for me.

It is hard for a man to ask for a favor. I did not wait for him to beg. It was the least I could do. Just take Jonas to the train station to wait for the underground. Perhaps I should have waited there longer. No matter. It is done. A man must do what a man must do.

He is in my wagon almost before it is stopped. His eyes search mine, but he does not speak. He must put his trust in me, for now he has no one else. **Don't worry, Jonas. We will make another contact. We have a little room at the top of the house. You will like it there.**

My shoes. *He whispers his first words for the lost shoes, but he is really asking for his father and mother, for his older brother, for his home and friends.*

We could not take a chance of those fine shoes in this old wagon. It is more important to keep people safe than to think about shoes. We will do our best. Everything will be all right.

The traffic is heavy. The uniforms look everywhere, searching for what they have forbidden. They do not watch me too closely as they like the farmers. They think I have taken my wheat to the mill. They do not know that the millstone is huddled on the seat just next to me.

The sunlight fades. Soon we will be near my village. What if one of my neighbors...? You cannot be sure about anyone these days. For over a hundred years my family has lived in the village, and just so for the families on each side, but the uniforms make us each mind our own tongues.

Jonas, now you will lie down in the soft hay. Sleep a little and we will soon be with my Helga. She will be happy to see you. Cover yourself like this so you will not be cold.

My wife will be happy to see you? Dummkopf, how could I say such a thing! My wife will be happy to share her food with you, to trudge up and down the stairs with water and a chamberpot? My wife will be happy to keep you secret from the other women in the village? My wife will be happy to be shot for hiding you?

But she is a good woman, Helga, my wife. If only God had seen fit to give us children, even one small child. If only God...

Jonas, I will stop for a moment near my house. I will tell my wife you will be our boy for a little while. Jonas, do not worry. These big bones of mine will protect you. Helga and I together will take care of you.

Helga, Helga, come quickly. There is a lost lamb, a little lost lamb.

There was a stunned silence when Allison finished reading the story. Women brushed away tears. Suddenly, applause swelled up. Allison nodded slightly as it continued.

Finally Josephine moved back to the podium and thanked Allison profusely. "I hope you will take some questions from the audience," she said. "I'm sure there will be quite a few."

"Is this a true story?" Someone asked.

Another said, "My sister and I were hidden during the war, too."

Allison answered each question or comment graciously, and before returning to her seat she was enveloped in one of Josephine's hugs. "Great presentation," Jo breathed into her ear.

Josephine turned to the group. "Your story, Allison, reminds us how one person's courage can make a real difference. Thank you so much for inspiring us. And many thanks to my wonderful committee, whose names are listed in your program.

"Although that story is a hard act to follow," Josephine continued, "I have the exciting details of our planned weekend retreat to the Monterey Health Spa. Rooms have been set aside for us for the weekend beginning Friday, May 9th through Sunday the 11th. It'll be a time to relax, eat healthy food, work out if you like and feel good. You'll be receiving further information and reservation forms in the mail. Thank you so much for being here today and lending your support to the BACC. And do enjoy the delicious lunch."

"The retreat sounds like fun," Maevis confided to Carol. "And

I'm sure my Neal won't mind caring for the kids for a weekend to give me some R & R."

"I've been to that spa," Carol answered. "You'll love it." *Maybe if I go, Felice will join me,* she thought. *She certainly could use some rest and relaxation.*

After dessert, when Allison was about to leave the ballroom, Josephine asked, "By the way, Allison, are you coming to the spa? I want you to drive down with me."

"Let me see what Brad thinks, and then we'll talk," Allison replied.

"I hope you can. And thanks again for today. You were wonderful."

"It did turn out well. I'm glad I let you talk me into it." She put on her brightest smile and tried to ignore the flatness she felt inside. "See you Saturday, the usual."

Josephine waited for the crowd to thin before beginning her own exit. As she made her way outside, she was stopped by the woman in the long flowered skirt and sandals.

"Josephine, great program! I'd love to go to the getaway retreat, but I'll need to catch a ride with someone. My old car won't make it over the hill, and I can never count on my friend Annie. Would I possibly be able to go with you? Do you live in San Jose? Can I chip in for gas?"

"Certainly," Josephine answered and handed Maevis her business card. "Give me a call."

Josephine marveled at the woman's ability to ask multiple questions without so much as a beat between them. *Let's see now,* she thought as she continued slowly to the parking lot. *There's Monique, and Allison if she comes, and this person and me. Four altogether. Quite a group.*

Everyone else had gone when Josephine reached her car. She sat down on the seat, swiveled, and lifted one leg at a time into driving position. The luncheon had been very successful. *An organizer, that's what I am. It's second nature. I can go from being on camera for the station to overseeing a major event like this, she commended herself.*

But why am I having so much trouble with my legs? And why do my hands feel numb?

Josephine chose not to dwell on those concerns. The luncheon had been perfect.

Two

"Hey, Nealsy! How would you like to spend an entire weekend of quality time with the kids? Just you and the kids, Neal, love. Doesn't that sound irresistible?" Maevis nudged him with her elbow. "I have the opportunity to go down near Carmel to soak up the sun for a few days with the women's charity group. Whattaya say?"

They lay together at the finish of their lovemaking. "Neal, did you hear me? You aren't asleep yet, are you?"

"I was," he groaned and shifted his weight. "Won't this keep until tomorrow?"

"No," Maevis smiled in the dark. "I have to get an answer now," she went on. "You know how easy it is to forget about things around here. And you're such a fantastic wonderful husband, not to mention a superb father, and..."

"Maaaeeeve, stop. Go to sleep." Neal turned away from his wife and curled up on his side.

"Nealsy, c'mon, say yes. I'll give you a whole weekend off for golf the next time Stefan invites you. Please?" She pursed her lips and kissed the empty air three times, sending him her love, their special signal for contentment.

Neal returned the pecks weakly into his pillow. "When is it?" he mumbled.

"In a few weeks. Our calendar's clear, I already looked. You'll only have to get Chloe to dance class and the twins to soccer. A piece of cake."

"Who are you going with?"

"The ladies from that luncheon I went to. Annie's group. They have a special rate at a spa for the weekend and it's super-reasonable."

"I'll let you know tomorrow, after I get some sleep. Quiet now. I have an early meeting."

"I'm going to interpret that as a 'yes,' my sleepy spouse." Maevis hugged him vigorously. "I told the women that you are just *too much.*" Maevis tucked her legs in behind his, her thighs pressed as tightly against him as they'd go and kissed him on whatever part of his back her lips met in the dark. "Love you, babe." She wrapped her arm around his torso and kissed him again, settling her head onto the pillow and closing her eyes.

⟫·◦·⟪

On Saturday morning Allison slid into the booth across from Josephine at the Sit 'n Sip coffee shop, greeting her friend as usual. "Hi, sweetie. What's new since I last saw you?"

"What's new?" Josephine repeated. "You're new, Allison. And I wish I could say 'shiny new,' but I can't believe you're the same perky lady who impressed everyone so much a couple of days ago at the luncheon."

Allison looked down and fiddled with her spoon.

Josephine continued. "You looked positively ravishing in that new green swishy dress, and here you are today in an old sweat suit and sneakers, looking droopy all over. What's going on?"

"Oh, this is just a neighborhood diner," Allison muttered. "There's no need to dress."

"Dress, bull!" retorted Josephine. "It's not only your clothes. The excitement of the luncheon took your mind off your heartache for a few hours, but now you're barely able to hold up your head. How can you have forgotten all your successes? Why aren't you beaming ear to ear?"

"What successes?" frowned Allison.

"Well, for one, the luncheon was a smash. Everyone who has ever heard you read about Jonas is impressed with your storytelling and says what an accomplished speaker you are. Then there are the thirty little kids who adore you as their teacher, not to mention your own kids — and Brad."

"Oh, Brad hardly knows I'm alive anymore! And our kids are mostly gone, out on their own. You know that."

Josephine took her friend's hand. "Look, Allison. I know that Brad loves you more than life itself, and you certainly can be proud of the way your blended family has turned out. And I love you! You're my best friend."

"I love you too, Jo, and your support means so much. You take such good care of me that I feel like you're my big sister, even though I'm older than you."

"Allison, pay attention. This is important." Josephine took a deep breath. "Today is the day I have to tell you what I've been mulling over for the past few weeks. You're a strong woman, but you've been feeling blue too long. It's time for you to see a professional."

Allison frowned again.

"This depression of yours is not passing," continued Josephine. "I asked around and got the names of two good shrinks. I want you to make an appointment with one of them and..."

"I don't need a shrink, Jo!" Allison interrupted. "I only need..." Allison couldn't finish the sentence.

"That's just it. You don't know what you need, Allison. Why, you've been so damn busy raising your three children ever since Alex left, and teaching school, and marrying Brad, and taking care of all five kids, that you've never had time to put your own soul at rest. Take these names and numbers and call one. For me."

Allison knew Jo wasn't going to take "no" for an answer, so she took the slip of paper and tucked it into her purse without answering. *Maybe I would enjoy a few hours talking to a good therapist in a dim, comfy room, she thought, where no one will interrupt, where I can let down my guard and just be me.*

That business tacitly agreed upon, the two friends ordered their favorite lunch of giant sautéed mushrooms and Caesar salad. Josephine mentioned the upcoming spa weekend and Allison realized she hadn't told Brad about it yet.

After the meal, Josephine wiped her mouth with her napkin and got up. "I'd better be heading back to work, but first I have to hit the restroom. Do you have time to pay the bill? Here's my half, sweetie." She kissed Allison's cheek. "Love you. Bye."

When Josephine came out of the bathroom, she hoped Allison had already gone and wouldn't see her leave the restaurant. Josephine walked slowly, holding onto the backs of the chairs for support. When she got outside, she suddenly stumbled and found herself sitting on the sidewalk.

The man from the newsstand rushed over.

"Miss, are you okay?" He helped her up.

"Thanks so much. I'll be fine." Josephine couldn't meet his gaze. *Lucky thing I wore these slacks today*, was all she could think. *Tough fabric. Any other would have torn.*

She looked down to see what she had tripped over, but there was nothing to see. *Why in the world did I fall?*

About fifteen minutes later Josephine pulled up and parked in front of her TV station. *My station.* That's how she thought of it. She was completely devoted to KTRS. She loved the work, the people, the news broadcasts, everything.

Josephine had started in television as an intern at KTRS during college and won a job there after graduation. Going into the world of television seemed natural for her, since she had been introduced to theater at an early age by her Aunt Danielle, and she'd gone on to work in high school and college productions in every capacity — costumes, lights, and acting. But it was the writing and directing that drew her the most.

KTRS appreciated her tenacity to see a story through, the ability to dig and ask penetrating questions. She had a good eye for camera work, too. Little by little, the station had given her more responsibility, until today she was one of its top reporters. She loved the work, except that most of the time she worked from three in the afternoon until ten at night in order to get the news reports ready for the evening broadcasts. Those hours left little time for a single woman's social life.

Josephine went into the editing room and slid a video into the machine. There on the screen was the tape she had made that morning of the aftermath of a gangfight in an East San Jose neighborhood. She was pleased with the way the clips of the mother of the boy who had been badly hurt, and the neighbors who were trying to comfort her, had turned out .

Josephine cut and spliced, then turned her attention to the teleprompter script that the announcer would be working from:

> Early this morning at 2:30 A.M. in front of the Seven/Eleven in the Mayfair section of San Jose, shots rang out. One young man was critically wounded and three others are being treated at the Santa Clara Valley Medical Center.

She would have to call the hospital and check on the boy's condition before the evening news broadcast. As she flipped through her rolodex for the hospital's phone number, the wall calendar with the tiny, colorful wildflowers caught her eye. Larry had given it to her. Larry. Whatever had become of him? A nice enough man, but the two of them simply hadn't clicked. He'd faded out of her life, and she had barely noticed. Maybe it was just as well.

Josephine turned back to the screen. Then Sam, the station manager, came in and looked over her shoulder at the monitor. He nodded approvingly.

"It looks good, Josephine."

"Thanks," she answered.

"And we're counting on you to get the Monday story on the South Bay Development Plan. Can you make it to the city council meeting?"

"Sure thing, Sam," Josephine replied confidently. Privately though, she wondered if she were going to be able to make it.

Her life seemed to have gotten a whole lot more complicated lately. She forced her attention back to the screen to finish the story and start the research for Monday's meeting.

Late that night, when sleep eluded her, the night demons took control again and fear swept over her. She knew that something was very wrong. The physician had said her symptoms were due to stress. Her hands felt like they had been in water too long and had lost their feeling. They couldn't hold onto things. Her legs felt like heavy slabs of concrete when she walked, and only Josephine knew that she was wearing a pad everyday because she was leaking. She was too embarrassed to share that with anybody, even Allison.

⊰•⊱

"Are you okay, Mrs. Boyce?" Allison's most sensitive second grader was standing at her elbow.

"Thank you for asking, Robbie. It's just a little headache. Do you need help with the worksheet, dear?" Allison walked him back to his desk.

That evening, Allison made an appointment with one of the psychologists whose names Jo had given her. At their first session, when the preliminaries were out of the way, Dr. Golman, the therapist, asked about Allison's first marriage.

"Oh, that was a long time ago," Allison shook her head dismissively.

"I know, but many of my patients have unresolved issues with their first love."

Allison shivered. "What can I say? We met, fell deeply in love, married, had kids," she hurried the words, "and lived the

American dream for many years. Then, WHAMMO! The big 'D'."

"How did you meet?"

"I was sixteen, a junior in high school. I was a bookworm, interested in academics only, not boys or hanky-panky. In our small town Alex's reputation for brains preceded him. One night I went to a fraternity dance with a boy named Sonny, and Alex and his date were in Sonny's car. The next day Alex came to find me. Here was a boy who was smarter than I was, and he had come looking for me. I was smitten.

"We started seeing each other often. I don't even remember where we went. Mostly we just talked." Allison looked at the therapist with teary eyes. "A picture of our two young heads together—discussing, learning, planning—is indelible in my memory. When we weren't in school, we couldn't stay away from each other. Everyone said 'Alex and Allie' as easily as they said 'peanut butter and jelly.'" Allison blushed.

Dr. Golman was writing in her notebook. "Go on," she encouraged.

"After high school, we were separated when he got a scholarship to the University of Southern California and I stayed behind to finish college in my hometown. I did my work and got involved in a few campus organizations, but it was hard. Our love for each other was intensified by the distance between us." Allison gazed at the wall. "For three and a half years we wrote voluminous letters. He would hitchhike the hundreds of miles back to see me whenever he could.

"We got married the day after my graduation. I looked forward to living happily ever after. We settled down in Los Angeles. He took the CPA exam, and no one was surprised when he came out first in the state. From then on he moved up from job to better job. As he got higher salaries, we moved into bigger houses. It was a storybook tale." She looked down at her hands. "The rest is history, as they say. A happy beginning and a nightmarish end. I was devastated."

Dr. Golman was quiet for a moment and then said gently, "Tell me about the divorce."

"The end came like a bullet. I was actually in bed, awaiting Alex's return from a late-night tax appointment when he came home, very pale.

"Honey, is something the matter?" I asked.

"I've had a hard day. I've decided to leave."

"'Oh, I'm sorry. Did you tell Sid?' was my naive reply. Sid was Alex's partner. He had started his own accounting firm years before with the backing of his father-in-law, and because Alex was so smart, Sid took him in as a full partner on the very first day," Allison explained, her face gleaming proudly, then falling as she got back to her story. "After a while, Alex thought he wanted to start another firm by himself. I thought almost nothing would surprise me anymore. But his answer hit me like a truck.

"He said, 'What has Sid got to do with this? I'm leaving you.'"

Allison wiped her nose and stared at the ceiling. "That's how it ended. I lost fifteen pounds in the first three weeks he was gone. I ran up a huge bill calling his Beverly Hills office begging him to come home so we could at least talk. When he finally came back, it was to take the kids out for pizza and to pick up the rest of his clothes.

"Alex, who used to tell me everything, never even told me why he left." Allison put the tissue away. "For the first time since I was sixteen, I didn't have Alex to rely on."

Shaken by the long-suppressed emotions revived in Dr. Golman's office, Allison wasn't ready to go home after the therapy session. She walked across the street to a small park and sat on a bench under a willow tree. *How did all that happen, Alex? We were supposed to be together for life, weren't we?*

Allison knew there were no answers. She also knew that what she had told the therapist wasn't the whole story. The end had been horrible, yes, but there had been so many good times. Especially in the beginning, when they were teenagers.

In those days, they could hardly keep their hands off each other. Sometimes when he came to pick her up they would clasp arms around each other and do an impromptu polka in her parents' living room in celebration of being together. Their time together was one of happiness for Allison and what was awaking in her; their time apart was a longing.

Whenever they could, they'd find a secluded spot to park. They were always hugging, kissing, and touching. Allison couldn't believe she was doing all this with a boy. But she didn't want to stop. Other girls were doing "it" she knew, but she had long before decided to wait until after marriage. She was more comfortable being tagged a "cold fish" than a "hot tamale," and Alex had respected her limits.

In the front seat of his car one night, she listened to the beat of his heart through his shirt. The thought came into her head that she wanted him to touch her. As she arched her back, his palm was there. His hand felt so good on her breast.

They sat for a long time, holding each other, not knowing what to do next. She did not dare to move. When he gently unbuttoned her blouse, undid her bra and then pulled his own shirt over his head, she did not protest. He gathered her to him and in that way they held each other.

Allison sighed and rose from the park bench. It was almost six o'clock. Time to go home. *I wonder if Brad will be available for a change. I want to talk to him about going to the spa, and I must remember to ask him if he came to the luncheon that day when I gave my speech. I'd be so happy to find out he cared enough to come.*

Three

I'm really going away. I must do it. Annie repeated the mantra to herself. *I must do it. I've got to free myself from the demands of the family.*

Annie hardly ever ventured out on her own, except to run errands or go to the skating rink. *This is crazy. How can I leave my husband and boys?* She looked into the well-stocked refrigerator. *What are they going to eat for dinner tonight? Will Steven remember to take his wet underwear out of the washer and put it in the dryer? This is ridiculous. I can't be worrying about them all the time. The boys are old enough to care for themselves for three days, for gosh sakes. I'm going to have a good time and meet new friends. And Maevis will be there.*

Annie always put her family first. She was comfortable being a homemaker just like her mother from the old country. Whenever her dear Mommalah would phone, the first question was always, inevitably, "What's cooking on the stove?" And how delighted her mother would be when Annie responded, "Mommalah, I've made your wonderful *cholent* recipe. Stanley just adores it."

Even though her boys, Steven and Darryl, were old enough to take care of themselves, Annie still catered to them. And she felt guilty if she didn't have a home-cooked meal prepared each night for Stanley when he got home from work.

Home was a safe haven for Annie. After high school she stayed close to her home in Oakland. She would take the city bus to Chabot College four times a week, but on weekends she'd head up to Berkeley to take folk dancing lessons.

Annie and Maevis had met in Berkeley at the Ashkenaz and then had rekindled their acquaintance two years ago in San Jose at the skating rink. Now they skated together regularly. It was one of Annie's rare breaks from domesticity.

Maevis would tell her over and over, "The boys are eighteen and twenty, Annie. They've reached adulthood. Your job is done. It's time you thought about yourself."

After the BACC luncheon, Maevis had insisted, "You just have to go to this women's retreat with me, Annie. It's going to be in Monterey County, not too far from here. We'll have a great time."

With Maevis' words ringing in her ears, Annie had finally agreed. She'd spent hours sorting through various outfits for the weekend. Now her overnighter was packed full. She tossed it into the back of the Toyota and hopped into the driver's seat. *Did I remember everything?* She fumbled with the seat belt. *I'm sure I could use an extra jacket, just in case it gets a little nippy at night.* She bounced out of the car and ran into the house to get her favorite all-weather purple and yellow parka. She spotted a straw sun visor in the closet. *I can probably use this, too. Did I pack sunscreen?* She grabbed a bottle of SPF 15 from the top of the refrigerator. *Just in case.*

Annie surveyed the kitchen. It was in reasonable order. *The boys are at school, Stan is at the clinic, and I am about to make my escape to the remote hills near Monterey. Should I take the frozen hamburger out to defrost? Nope. I'm not going to pamper them.*

Annie hurried out of the house with all her paraphernalia before the magnetic forces in the kitchen could draw her back. Once again she bounded into the car and strapped herself in, determined not to budge until she arrived at the spa. About six blocks from the house a thought crossed her mind. *Oh, my God, did I turn off the stove?* She forced herself not to panic; she took deep breaths and convinced herself that the stove was surely turned off.

Fifteen miles from home her mind was still racing with worry and guilt. *How will Stan and the boys cope without me?* She turned on the radio to her favorite oldies but goodies station. A Simon and Garfunkel tune was playing, and Annie started humming as she motored down Highway 101 going south. She rolled the window halfway down, and the light breeze swept through her curls. Singing the words about being a rock and being an island, Annie felt her anxiety finally dissipate. The song ended, but Annie kept humming. She heard herself say aloud, "I don't give a frick if I come home to wilted lettuce and an untouched tuna casserole. I'm so glad Maevis convinced me to go away this weekend." With the car in overdrive, Annie began to enjoy the ride.

———

Allison was having second thoughts. First, she had let Jo talk her into being a speaker at the luncheon and then into seeing a shrink, and now she was going away for a whole weekend with a group of women she hardly knew. As Allison packed, she found herself hoping that the hippie woman from the luncheon wasn't going to be there. Of course, the Maevis person wouldn't admit she had been a hippie, but Allison knew it the minute she had seen her at the luncheon with her long earrings and flowing skirt bearing down on Josephine. Maevis certainly looked like a card-carrying hippie, only a hop, skip and jump out of the Berkeley scene of the sixties. Allison could just picture her running up and down with a placard, protesting some seemingly important world ill, long hair flying, probably with her toothbrush and birth control pills tossed into a filthy knapsack. A vision of free life and free love. It repelled Allison. She had always chosen the responsible side of the street.

Allison carefully selected the clothes she would take to the spa and tried to bank on the hope that Maevis wouldn't be going with the group. Perhaps Maevis would be unable to get away from her pack of young ones. Allison wondered why this particular woman bothered her so much. Why was she, Allison, who was usually open to different viewpoints, suddenly put off so much by her brief encounter with Maevis? In truth, Allison had long ago grown to admire many of the political and social beliefs first espoused by the flower children. But there was no way she could embrace Maevis.

Allison packed a swimsuit and a shorts set she had purchased some weeks ago. She examined her motives for signing up for this mini-vacation. First, of course, to be with Josephine. And second, she knew she deserved at least one weekend for herself. She looked forward to being pampered, massaged, exercised and fed, in the company of interesting women, and to being in bed at night alone with her own thoughts.

Four of the kids were away at college or on their own now. She and Brad had five youngsters between them when they met and rushed from their respective divorces into the security of a second marriage. The two of them had centered their lives on raising the children, and now only Kevin remained at home for a few more months before he would be off to university. Some people thought she had married Brad just to have a husband and father in the house. But that wasn't it at all. She loved Brad. It was easy to rely on him. He could do anything and everything. In fact, he was the warmest and most capable man she had ever known.

One day shortly after they were married, Brad surprised her by buying a used motor home so they could take the entire family on trips. They'd had so much fun setting up campsites, doing the work and then playing together afterward. Brad was always upbeat and enthusiastic. He also made her feel loved and wanted.

Things had changed though. In the last six months it seemed to Allison that Brad didn't even notice if she was there. Her once loving, attentive husband had recently sold his business to a larger corporation and now spent all his time at his computer in the back of the house. She had grown so accustomed to Brad's nurturing that she was hurt and angry when she walked into the computer room and he barely looked up from his screen. She felt abandoned all over again.

Yes, the kids had almost all left and Brad was holed up either at his computer or in his workshop. She knew there was a name for the way she was feeling — empty nest syndrome — they called it. But Allison never thought it would hit her. She had so many other interests — her teaching, volunteering, playing bridge with the ladies, and her friendship with Jo. Surely this spa weekend couldn't have come at a better time. Brad would miss

her so much it would put new *oomph!* into their marriage.
Besides, what could she lose except a few pounds?

⊰⊱

Feeling exhilarated and carefree, Annie remembered that there
were discount clothing shops just off the highway in Gilroy. *Maybe
I'll stop and buy a pair of shoes to match my special purse.* When
she saw the freeway sign indicating the outlet stores, she exited
and pulled into the parking lot. She was amazed at how quickly
she found the perfect pair of pumps for a mere $150. *These will
look great with the anniversary bag that I bought myself in San
Francisco. How could I ever forget the eventful day when I made
that purchase? Stanley had his cardiologist conference in the city,
and I'd decided to tag along to buy myself something in celebration of our 23rd wedding anniversary, which naturally Stanley
forgot.*

*I really couldn't have cared less about handbags, but I real-
ized I had never shopped for a divine purse, the kind that most
women would die for. I walked into Saks 5th Avenue and headed
for the purse department without hesitation. I found a clearance
table marked 30% - 50% off and felt that was a safe place to look
when you don't know what you're looking for. I didn't dare ask a
salesclerk for assistance for fear of being discovered as a virgin
purse shopper. I checked several purses for durability, color and
style. I was hoping to find the one purse I truly, deeply fell madly in
love with and had to take home, regardless of the price— unless it
was over $60. I picked up several purses from the clearance table,
but none gave me that rush I was looking for. I almost settled for
an olive green leather one with a wide strap. I draped it over my*

shoulder to see if it fit comfortably. The price was right. It was reduced from $100 to $50. What a bargain! But had I fallen in love with it? Maybe it took more time. Should I buy it?

I sensed the saleswoman was becoming curious about me. I had been in the department for almost an hour without selecting anything. Then, lo and behold, I spotted the perfect purse. Immediately — did she have a sixth sense?— the saleslady approached and told me she had a fresh one in the back room. While waiting, I kept fondling this incredible, but simple purse. I knew it would be absolutely practical for summer and part of fall. White, with strands of purple, yellow and blue braided on the trim, the purse would complement all my outfits.

*I had almost persuaded myself to buy it when the saleslady came out of the stockroom and handed me an untouched one, still in the protective plastic wrapping. "It was $300, but fortunately, it is on sale today for a mere $199," she announced. I tried to conceal my dismay, but the strong smell of leather and the smooth texture inside and out made it hard to resist. It was the moment of truth for me. Could I feel justified in buying such a costly creation? Yes! I handed the lady my credit card. After all, it **was** my anniversary.*

Now, in the Gilroy outlet, Annie realized that it would be just as easy for her to love this exquisite pair of shoes as it was to love that anniversary purse. But before leaving the shopping center, she called home to make sure the stove was turned off. Then, with her new shoes in tow, she was off to the spa, glad that she had made the decision to splurge.

Felice was not one to miss an opportunity to network with the professional women from the BACC. She called around and found that several of her colleagues were planning to go on the weekend retreat. Scheduled for May, it was far enough ahead for Felice to make arrangements to be out of the office that Friday. She penciled the date on her calendar and punched in her secretary's extension. "Don't make any appointments for me on Friday, May 9th. I'll be out of the office for that day and the rest of that weekend."

She remembered that one of her mother's friends had taken Carol to the same spa several months after Daddy died. Every time Felice thought about her father being dead, something gripped her in the chest. One day he was busy at his desk, the next day he was gone. It had happened so suddenly. And he was barely sixty, certainly not old these days. Sometimes she thought her loss was even greater than her mother's. After all, her mother might marry again. But she, Felice, would never have another father.

Felice picked up the phone again, this time to call her mother. She was determined to get Carol out of the house. Carol sounded excited about the idea of going to the spa. "I've always wanted to go back, but I never had the opportunity. I'll be happy to go with you, Felice."

There, thought Felice. *I was right. Mother isn't capable of doing anything by herself. Why, if I hadn't mentioned it to her, the woman would never have thought of taking a weekend at the spa. She needs my guidance.*

"I loved the place, the views are beautiful," Carol was rambling on. "The Japanese touches are so tranquil, and just to sit around the pool and look over at the mountains was pure joy.

The cabins are small, as I remember, too small for two adults. There are some newer rooms, too. We'll each take a separate room and we'll have our privacy."

"Oh, you think that's best? Well, alright." Felice hadn't given the room situation any thought, and since her mother had been there before, maybe she knew best this once.

A week before the planned retreat Carol telephoned Felice and told her she intended to drive. Felice was surprised. It was unusual for her mother to make a definite statement like that. Felice had detected changes in her mother lately, an independent streak she had never seen when her father was alive. But she still doubted her mother's ability to make wise decisions and was furious with her latest idea of wanting to sell the house.

"No, Mother, I'm a better driver, and besides, I'm looking forward to going over the mountains in my new Porsche."

"I know you, Felice," Carol shot back, "you'll be working long hours trying to get everything lined up for your secretary to take care of on the one day you'll be out of the office. You won't be rested. I'll do the driving."

Felice found her mother immovable. Well, if it made Carol happy to drive, that was a little thing to give in to.

———◆———

Josephine wondered how *she* had been elected to drive this awful mountain road. *Oh, right. Now I remember.* No one else had offered to drive, so with her usual bravado, Josephine had taken charge. *'No problem. I'll drive.' Those were my very words.*

Oddly, Sam had encouraged her when she'd asked for the three days off. He switched her weekend schedule with a coworker, Diane. Josephine was glad to get away from the pressure of the deadlines at the TV station, grateful for the opportunity to unwind. And she needed to sort out some disturbing things that were happening to her, things she did not understand.

Allison was miserable in Jo's car. She was virtually imprisoned next to Maevis in the back seat. Allison had been trained to be a lady at all times and to make the best of any bad situation that she could not alter. But no sooner had Allison buckled her seat belt than Maevis started interrogating everyone. "Was it hard for you to get away for the weekend? Do you think we can survive on only 1200 calories a day? Did you ever have a massage? How many children do you have?"

Josephine didn't have any children, Monique had one daughter, and Maevis wanted to tell all about her own three. Then Maevis just couldn't get over the fact that Allison had five children. Maevis asked so many questions about it that Allison finally had to explain.

"They aren't all from the same litter. Some are mine and some are my husband's."

"Oh, so you're divorced and remarried? Or were you widowed?"

That was too much for Allison. She didn't like Maevis and didn't want to reveal her life history. She shrugged and turned her face toward the window. Monique, sensing the tension between the two women in the back, quickly spoke up.

"Josephine, your straw hat on the dashboard reminds me of something that happened when I arrived here from France in 1946. Would you all like to hear about it?" She turned around and smiled, but Allison was still staring out of the side window and Maevis was picking at her fingernail.

"We'd love to hear about it," responded Josephine.

"Yes, we certainly could use a little diversion right about now," came from Allison.

Monique shifted around in her seat to better include the women in the back, and began her story. "You might have guessed by my speech that I'm from France."

"I thought so!" Maevis shouted. "I'm good at placing accents."

"When I first met my husband Andrew — before he was my husband, of course —" Monique laughed, "he was a GI over in Algeria, in North Africa. I had fled there with my family during the war. When the war was finally over and VE Day arrived — Victory in Europe is what they called it — Andrew was discharged and he was going to return home to Chicago. We were in love and had become engaged by then, and I was heartbroken when I found out that we were to be separated for nine months."

"How awful," Allison commiserated, "that must have been unbearable for you. Why couldn't you go back with him?"

"You see," Monique answered, "all available ships and planes were being used to transport American military back to the United States. We civilians had to wait. Finally, I was able to book passage to join him in America. Naturally, my protective French mother accompanied me."

"Of course," Allison nodded. "You couldn't let a young, unmarried girl cross the ocean unchaperoned in those days."

"Well, when we arrived in New York, an old friend of the family offered to put us up for a few days until we could leave for Chicago, where Andrew was awaiting my arrival. Our friend

Siegfried, was a refugee from Germany and had arrived in New York some years earlier. His trade was hat-making and his business was thriving.

"'You need to arrive in Chicago with a hat more up-to-date than the one you are wearing,' Monique imitated his thick German accent. 'Your fiancé's family will want you to look more American and less French. I am going to make you a hat that they will love.'

"'But, Siegfried,' I protested, 'I adore my felt *cloche* with its long feather on the side.' Who was I, however, to contradict the expert on women's hats in America? So, I let him make me a new hat, and then I took off with my mother for Chicago and my beloved fiancé."

"How did you travel?" Josephine asked.

"By train," Monique responded. "And the train was so modern to me. Not like the ones I had been on in Europe. There was actually a small room attached to our compartment where we could watch a movie. A movie on a train! I couldn't believe it. I was very excited during our journey, which took almost twenty-four hours."

"A whole day to get there?" Maevis asked loudly.

"Yes. My heart was pounding as we got closer to Chicago. I was thinking that I would soon be held and kissed by the man I had dreamt about for so long. My Andrew would be there waiting for me, his 'French import,' as he liked to refer to me in his letters.

"Finally, Chicago! I spent the last hour putting on make-up and fixing my hair so that the curls would bounce on either side of my new hat."

"Monique, that's so cute!" Maevis called out.

"I was wearing the new creation made by Siegfried. Covered by a crown of daisies, it sat on my head like a flowerpot."

"Goodness!" Josephine exclaimed.

"My mother and I stepped down from the train. I carried my French felt hat in its round box.

"'Voilà Andrew, Maman!' I shouted. 'There is Andrew!' Indeed, Andrew came running towards us and embraced me. But instead of kissing me he whispered into my ear, 'Please take off that awful hat! My family is waiting at the end of the platform and I don't want them to meet you wearing a portable garden on your head.'"

The car was filled with laughter. Maevis stomped her feet, yelling, "That's too much!"

"Oh," said Monique regretfully, "I should have kept my Parisian hat and not tried to be something I was not."

"I can almost picture the hat Siegfried made you, *ma pauvre chérie.*" Josephine liked to practice her college French on Monique.

Monique's cheeks were pink. She hoped she had managed to both distract and entertain, and that the others were not just being polite.

"Well, ladies," Maevis spoke up again, "I don't have an amusing story to tell, but I'd like to make a contribution, okay?" She leaned forward and looked at Josephine and Monique for the go-ahead.

"Sure," Jo answered, keeping her eyes on the road. "What is your 'contribution'?"

Maevis fumbled in her backpack and passed an audio cassette forward. "Go ahead, Monique," Maevis urged her. "Put it in, right into that slot," she pointed, "and then turn up the volume."

Monique inserted the tape. A sharp drum roll filled the car.

"Oh, damn it!" Allison gritted her teeth and turned to stare out of the side window again.

"Yeah!" Maevis yelped excitedly. " 'Just let me hear some of that rock and r-o-o-o-ll music... any ol' time you choose it...,'" Maevis sang along in her twangy alto. "My sweet brother-in-law put together this compilation tape especially for me. He knows all my favorite songs."

She drummed on the inside of the car door and bounced in time to the beat. "'Gotta be rock 'n roll music, if you wanna dance with me... if you wanna dance with me... if you wanna dance with me...' Boom, boom, boom! Yeah! I *love* that one!"

"I don't know about you, Jo," Allison said as the uproar ended, "but when I'm driving, I have trouble concentrating on the road if there's loud music playing."

"It's okay, Allison," Josephine said. "According to these directions we're almost there. It should be about a mile down this turnoff." Jo maneuvered the vehicle onto a tree-lined frontage road. "I think I see a sign up ahead."

"Oh, I love this song, too!" Maevis shimmied her shoulders as "Johnny B. Goode" started. "Chuck Berry," she noted over the sound of the music. Allison blew her nose and slumped down in the seat.

"We used to dance to these songs in junior high during lunch. Girls with girls, naturally," Maevis explained to no one in particular. "Anybody here know how to jitterbug?"

Monique turned around and nodded at her. Maevis laughed.

"I can't imagine that you French kids did much boogeying to Motown hits."

"Actually," Monique replied, "my girlfriends and I went dancing with the G.I.'s quite often in Algiers."

"Did your mother have to come along?" kidded Josephine as she pulled onto a gravel driveway leading uphill. She turned off the engine in a small parking area near an intricately carved magnificent Japanese-style bamboo gate, plain but elegant. A gravel path led to a weatherbeaten brown-shingled cottage with a sign that read Office.

"We made it!" Josephine announced gaily. "And what a relief, too. I'd forgotten how much I dislike that road over the mountains."

"Thank you so much, Josephine, but…" Monique spoke hastily, opening the passenger door and gathering up her two small suitcases. "…I must hurry to find a restroom. I'll see you inside."

"You did a superb job, Josephine," Allison called forward to her friend. "You must be exhausted."

Josephine pressed the eject button, removed the cassette, and handed it backwards over her shoulder. "Here, Maevis. You don't want to forget your brother-in-law's tape, do you?"

"No way! I need it for my jogging. And speaking of, I'm ready for a run right now. Thanks for the lift, Josephine. Bye everyone, see you later!" Maevis dropped the tape into her bag, swung the bag over her shoulder, and was out of the car, trotting away in a flash.

"Boy, she's a kick," Jo smiled wearily.

"Kicks like that I can do without," Allison added abruptly.

Josephine pulled herself out of the car and looked at the slight uphill slope of the walkway with concern. Would she be able to walk it without stumbling?

"Can I help you with your bag?" Allison asked, looking at her friend with a worried expression.

"No need, sweetie. I'll manage," Jo answered. She looked around. Her gaze took in a hot tub embedded on the terraced hillside that bloomed with masses of flowers, overlooking Carmel Valley and rolling hills in the distance. Through large trees with thick trunks and heavy foliage that shaded the area, Josephine got glimpses of the guest cabins.

"Come on," she said eagerly to Allison. " Let's see what awaits us."

Four

M onique went quickly to the office and left her suitcases with the young woman at the desk, explaining that she had a reservation and would check in shortly. The unpleasantness in the van during the trip had made her uncomfortable, and she was glad to be outside. Monique had been an "éclaireuse," a French girl scout, and she loved the outdoors. Now she was ready to take any road. A little wooden arrow pointed out the trail leading to Vista Point, and Monique followed the path.

The smell of the wildflowers and pine trees reminded her of the village in Normandy to which she and her family had first fled. They left Paris in 1939 and went north with all their belongings, fearing that their city would be bombed by the Nazis. The blue flowers along this path now reminded Monique of her father's small garden in the backyard of that rented house near the beach. A great abundance of blue-purple anemones had grown there, and the landlord harvested them to bring in a few extra francs for himself.

But as the Nazis marched through Belgium, her family had found itself once again in the path of danger. This time they escaped south in a small Citroen, leaving everything behind but her mother's Persian rugs and Meissen dolls, which they packed into the trunk of the car. When they were able to return to their former home in Normandy after the war, they stared at vacant rooms with empty picture frames on the walls. The Germans had cut out all the original paintings and sent them home to their families. The landlord, assuming that Monique's family would never return, had helped himself to their good furniture.

Mon Dieu! Monique was rushing along the trail. *Slow down, you're not a young woman anymore,* she reminded herself. *And it has been more than forty years since we lived in that little house in Normandy.* Monique thought now of her Papa always saying, *"La vie est belle!"*— in spite of all their troubles.

———◆◆———

After buying the shoes, Annie drove for another hour. She stopped at a service station for some unleaded supreme and a Baby Ruth bar. Her hair, which she had stuck under the bathroom faucet to give it the right shape, was still damp, and her glasses were smudged from facial lotion she hadn't had time to wipe off her hands. But she was feeling less and less like a runaway homemaker escaping from the drudgery of crumby floors and a leaky refrigerator, and more like a free agent. *I can't believe I've been a slave to that ancient fridge for so long. As soon as I get back, a new side-by-side with ice maker for me!* Annie admitted to herself that she'd become too attached to that first purchase, made when she and Stan were newlyweds.

Annie approached the gate to the spa and eagerly surveyed the area. *I'm glad there are no plastic pink flamingos decorating these grounds. I should get rid of ours and replace them with some terra cotta squirrels at least.* She parked her gray station wagon in the designated area and stepped out. The view overlooked a valley with scattered groves of coast redwoods. Annie was pleasantly absorbed in her surroundings and didn't notice Maevis approaching.

"Yay, Annie! I'm so glad you're here." Maevis spun her around and gave her a rib-busting bear hug.

"Did you bring your rollerblades, Maev?" Annie joked when she recovered her breath.

"You betcha!" Maevis laughed. "Well, I've got my jogging shoes, for sure."

Annie and Maevis shared hot fudge sundaes at the neighborhood skating rink in San Jose and rehashed stories of their Berkeley days while jogging together. At the rink, Annie wore old-fashioned skates with wheels, while Maevis had moved on to the newer rollerblades.

"Have you had a chance to look around? Don't you love this place already?" Maevis asked. "Put on your Reeboks and meet me here in fifteen minutes for a quick one."

Annie entered the office. Josephine and Allison were standing in an alcove. They turned to her as she headed for the registration desk.

"Are you here for the BACC retreat?"

"Why yes, I am," Annie responded.

"I'm Josephine." The rosy-cheeked woman offered her hand. "And this is Allison. She's a schoolteacher playing hookey."

Annie smiled. "I'm Annie Ross and I've just become a liberated housewife. I'm doing my own thing, though I'm not sure what that is yet."

"Good for you!" Allison gave Annie a pat on the back. "We're all here to find ourselves or to lose a few pounds. Lunch is in a little while. Join us in the dining room?"

"Whoopie, lunch!" replied Annie. "I'm ready. But I have a friend here with me. Can I bring her?"

"Of course," Josephine and Allison dueted.

Annie registered and found her cabin. She unpacked the paisley overnighter. The single room with a bath was small but comfortable. There was an arrangement of flowers in a Japanese vase on the dresser. The wallpaper matched the curtains. Directly outside the window was a profusion of poppies, and a swimming pool. Annie was sweaty and the pool looked inviting, but Maevis would be expecting her to run.

Annie took out three pair of red shorts with elastic waistbands and several undergarments with the days of the week embroidered on them. She stuffed a dresser drawer with her panties, nightie, swimsuit and shorts. She hung her blouses neatly in the closet. *Finally, a room of my own,* she marveled. *This is worth the whole trip.* She changed clothes, laced up her running shoes and hurried out to find Maevis.

———◆◆◆———

Carol picked up Felice early that Friday morning so they could make a rest stop along the way and still get to the spa before lunch. As soon as Felice got into the car she began a harangue about why Carol should not sell her house. "You can't buy a house half as nice for twice the money these days, and besides, Mother, that's *my* home, too. That's where you and I and Daddy always lived."

For a minute, Carol drove without answering. Then she said firmly, "I don't want to talk about this with you anymore, Felice. I will think about it before I do anything, but it's too much house for just me, and in the end, I have to do what's best for me."

After that rebuke, Felice hardly spoke. *At least we're not quarreling,* Carol thought. When they arrived at the spa and entered the office to check in, Felice saw an acquaintance of hers, another lawyer with whom she hoped to confer. She went to greet her. She hardly noticed that Carol had taken care of the registration and was standing next to her with their cabin keys. "We're across the walkway from one another," Carol said when her daughter's colleague left, handing Felice a key. "Close enough."

In her room, Felice pulled out a folder of notes she intended to work on over the weekend for a pending case of an unmarried twenty-year-old mother. The young woman's parents were seeking custody of her nine-month-old child, their grandchild. It was a typical case for Felice, who specialized in custody and divorce cases, and she gave each one her meticulous attention. Her father had noticed Felice's logical mind and ability to retain details. When he realized that she wasn't going to marry, he had encouraged her to pursue a career in law that would guarantee her independence and a good income. Felice knew instinctively that she would specialize in family law, defending the rights of women and children.

Felice's parents pinned their hopes and expectations on her, their only child. They beamed with pride the day she received her law degree. While working on an early case, Felice had met Sylvie, and they'd become fast friends. Felice knew her mother grieved that she would probably never give her grandchildren, but Carol had accepted Sylvie gradually, and they had grown to be genuinely fond of each other.

⸺⸺⸺

What fun, thought Jo. *We all managed to leave obligations behind to be here for two whole days.* She glanced around the sunlit glass-enclosed dining solarium. There were large pots with fan palms surrounded by pink impatiens and cascading lobelia. Josephine was glad she had convinced Allison to sit with her for lunch. Allison had balked because Maevis was there at the table with Annie. But Allison soon gave in to Jo's pleading, not wanting to cause a scene.

Carol and Felice entered the dining room together. "Look, there's room for both of us over there," Carol pointed to the long table where the others sat. "That's my friend Monique. And that's Maevis, the woman I talked to at the luncheon. Let's sit with them," she suggested to her daughter.

Felice turned to look for her own friends, but decided it would be a better idea to get her mother settled first with the people Carol knew. Then she'd be free.

"Carol!" Maevis shouted and jumped up. "I'm so happy to see you again. Come sit next to me, like before. What have you been up to since we met at the luncheon? Still knitting?" she laughed.

Felice moved away from her mother and walked to where Allison was sitting next to Josephine. She leaned over Allison's shoulder and said in an attempt at a whisper, "I almost didn't recognize you at the luncheon. You certainly have changed.

Remember me?"

Allison didn't know how to respond. Was that a compliment? "Oh, hello F... Felice," she stammered. "How've you been? It's nice to see you. I... I always meant to thank you... for..."

"No need, Allison. None at all. Lawson and Montgomery is known to be the best at what we do." Felice nodded matter-of-factly, waived two fingers at Carol and left.

Josephine had her fork poised over the delicate salad arrangement after she'd made a few introductions. She looked around at the other women seated at the table. *A private get-together later in my room is called for. I'll mention it to them after we eat.* "What did you think of those hors d'oeuvres?" she asked the others. "Weren't they something else?"

"This food is fantastic," exclaimed Carol. "I loved it last time I was here too. Would you believe, someone I spoke to over there told me she's been here for three weeks and has lost sixteen pounds? Imagine losing that much!"

"It is delicious food," Monique said. "And I can't tell this is low-calorie. Can you?"

"No way. It's too good," cooed Maevis. "I wish I had someone to cook for me like this everyday at home. Healthy gourmet, I call it."

"I don't know whether to eat this millet pilaf or graze on it." Annie stared at her plate of mixed grains with spiced vegetables. "Maybe there's a piece of filet mignon hidden underneath?" She started poking at the food with her fork.

"Annie, we're at a health spa, not a barbecue," Allison told her. "Drink up your potassium. You'll feel rejuvenated by the end of the weekend."

"If you don't die of starvation first," Maevis nudged Annie.

Annie stuffed herself but was not sure what she was eating. She finally felt a part of the vegetarian world, among the health-conscious, meatless-eating breed. The entreé she had consumed provided her with a sensual experience. Her taste buds were enhanced, her nasal passages cleared. "I wish I could get Stan and the boys off the red stuff," she said. "Once I camouflaged leftover rice with baked broccoli flowerlets and cauliflower au gratin. I tried to pass it off as a Julia Child concoction, giving it a fictitious name. I was taught by another newlywed early in my marriage that if you fry onions with your leftovers, the smell will compensate for the look. But when it was time to sample the mishmash, Stanley blurted out, 'What the heck is this?' and he wouldn't touch it!"

There was a lot of laughter at the table. Annie held up her empty glass. "This drink was so bad," she announced to the group, "but I'm hooked on the grains."

"What kind of activities are there for the afternoon?" Monique asked Josephine.

"According to this list," Josephine answered, reading a green paper, "there is aquasize class right after lunch and yoga at two." She passed the schedule to Monique.

Monique looked it over. "Did you know there are evening activities, too?" She showed the list to Carol, who was sitting on her left.

"Look," Carol pointed. "An instructor from the University of California Santa Cruz Extension is giving a journaling class tonight."

"Oh, I'm going to that!" Maevis said. "I love to write. Did I tell you I've been keeping a diary since I was eleven, Carol?"

Suddenly Jo called out, "Attention, everybody. How about a little get-together in my room later — before dinner?" She lowered her voice. "I've sneaked in some red and white wine and a few other goodies, in case you haven't had your daily quota of calories."

"That's a splendid idea," Monique said.

Carol nodded. "I'll be there."

"Count us in," Maevis turned to Annie. "Okay with you?"

"Sure!" Annie stood up. "Anyone interested in checking out the rest of this Shangri-la? I need to walk off that hearty meal."

"I'll join you," Monique said. "But first I need to go to my room for a visor and sunscreen."

Carol put down her teacup and leaned across to Maevis. "Are you going to the pool for water exercises?" she asked.

"Yes ma'am!" Maevis rose. "I'll get into my bikini and see you there in about fifteen minutes. We can get in some warm-up laps before the class starts. Bye all!"

Carol turned to Allison. "How about joining Maevis and me?"

Allison's reply was instant and tart. "No thanks," she answered. "I hate the water."

Carol was puzzled. *This is going to be an interesting weekend,* she thought.

"I may go to yoga later," Josephine said. Then she smiled, her eyes blazing with a devilish twinkle. "Don't forget, Carol. We all have a date at four in my room."

"I won't forget," Carol replied. "I'm looking forward to it. See you then."

"Excuse me, Allison," Josephine said as she pulled herself

up from the table. "I saw a display of herbal remedies in the lobby when we first came in. I'd like to check them out. I know you mentioned going on a bike ride, but can you come over before the get-together — at about 3:30 — to help me set up?" Allison nodded her assent.

Josephine had wanted to investigate the use of herbs for a long time, but never made it a top priority. Now there they were, conveniently displayed. Maybe she would find something that might help her current problems. She started to read the labels to learn as much as she could.

"Here's a fact sheet that explains these herbs," said a deep voice.

Josephine looked up into the face of the speaker. He had a tumble of short black curls, dark eyes, and a slight stubble of beard on his cheeks and chin. A nice chin, she noted, and a very sensible nose.

"Thank you," Josephine said, taking the paper he offered. She tried to read it but felt his stare. She looked up again. He was openly studying her face.

"The herbs are grown not far from here," he began, finding his voice again, "and they are very pure. What are you looking for?"

"What am I looking for?" Josephine repeated. She glanced down blankly at the paper and then back at him. "I don't know yet. I have an idea, but I'm not sure." She paused and then added, "I'm tired a lot."

His eyebrows knit together. "There are several things that can raise your energy level without side effects. I have used them myself and on our guests."

Our guests? she thought. *Does he work here or run this place? Or own it?* She watched him carefully select several small bottles. He told her about each one, how and when to take it, and what she could expect. She was impressed with his knowledge and liked the easy way he explained everything to her.

"Although I know quite a bit, it's best to speak to a professional herbalist," he added. "I have the phone number of one who lives close by, if you want." He smiled at her. "By the way, I'm Jack."

"Thanks, Jack. I'm Josephine. And yes, I'll take that number. I have a long way to go to grasp what herbs are all about."

"They're not too difficult to figure out," he said in a reassuring voice.

"You certainly seem to know a lot," Josephine said. "How did you get so smart?"

"My father had a stroke when I was in high school, and he wound up in a wheelchair. I wanted to help take care of him, so I learned everything I could about vitamins and herbal remedies. I like to think I prolonged his life a bit."

"What a great thing to do for your dad! Your mother must have appreciated the help."

Jack shrugged. "My mom tried to understand what I was doing, but I don't think she tried too hard. Actually, she had a busy life of her own with all her activities and clubs, and that gave me more time to spend with dad."

Josephine's TV reporter genes kicked in and she found herself asking for more. "You must have loved him a lot. What was he like?"

"He was a born teacher and loved his trade as he used to call it," Jack beamed. "I can remember students coming to our house at all hours to talk to him, or he would take them on special field trips. He was gentle, but could be strict when he needed to be."

Jack came back to the present. He gazed at Josephine intently. "Enough about me. I have the feeling I've seen you before."

"A lot of people say that," said Josephine, not willing to divulge that he might have seen her on TV, "but this is my first trip to a spa."

"I'm sure you'll enjoy it here," he smiled. They stood looking at each other. "If you're stressed," Jack resumed, "why not get a massage during your stay? That always helps."

"Thanks. I may do that also."

He pointed to a table at the other end of the lobby. "The sign-up sheet is over there."

"You seem to know a lot about this resort. Do you work here?" she finally asked him.

"My mother owns the place." Now he smiled more broadly, showing even white teeth.

"Really?" Josephine exclaimed. Another interviewer question bubbled up. "For how long?"

"So you want the whole story, huh?" Jack teased. "Well, when my dad died about ten years ago, Mom took the insurance money and bought this spa. I don't know what possessed her to do that, but she had come here many times, always loved the Carmel area and was sick of Marin county, where we'd lived before. So when the property became available, she went for it."

"Did you come too?"

"For a little while, but I left for college pretty soon after that."

"I'll bet you studied health there," Josephine ventured.

"Not right away," Jack began but then stopped. "It's a long story, Josephine, and I don't want to take up your whole afternoon. Let's leave it for another time. I'll be seeing you around again, I'm sure."

She watched him as he passed by, smoothly and effortlessly. He moved behind the lobby desk and through an archway beyond it, turning just before he disappeared to look again at Josephine, who returned his smile.

Five

Allison hurried back to her room after lunch, but on the path outside the cabins she was stopped by someone she didn't know. "Weren't you the speaker at the Children's Council luncheon a few weeks ago?" the woman asked. "Your story about Jonas and the Dutch farmer really touched me. You're a very good speaker. You should make a career of lecturing."

"Oh, thanks," Allison laughed. "But with my marriage, five kids and thirty more in the classroom, I have a full plate," she answered.

A few minutes later in the shower, with warm water dripping down her back and her eyes closed, Allison sighed. *If my plate is so full, then why am I feeling so empty?* She let the water course onto her upturned face. After toweling off, she changed into a white polo shirt and a pair of shorts, hoping to change her mood along with her clothes. *To hell with Maevis. And Felice, too,* she told herself as she slammed the door, checked that it was locked, and turned to face the day. She headed for a stand of bicycles stacked against the office wall for use by the spa guests. *That's what I'll do, I'll take off by myself on a bicycle.*

It had been years since Allison was on anything but a

stationary bike, and she felt exhilarated when she mounted and pushed down on the pedal and wheeled off. *A day like this just begs for a bike ride, and I need to do something physical. The sky is blue, the air smells clean, the sun is keeping me warm from the breezes, and I'm going to enjoy myself — no matter what.*

She rolled by some tall cedars, the sun's rays peeking through the branches. She stretched her legs as she pumped to reach the top of an incline. "Oh, what a beautiful morning," Allison yodeled, knowing full well that it was afternoon and that she was slightly off-key. *Gosh, I'm working muscles I haven't used in years.* She braked at the first glimpse of the ocean. *How I wish Jo were here with me! Or Brad. This scene is a sight for city-weary eyes. It cleanses my soul. I feel as free as the white bird soaring and dipping overhead.* She took a few more deep breaths. *I feel like I'm getting a hug from the whole world.*

<hr />

At 3:30, Allison went to her friend's cabin. "What should I put these nuts in?" she asked Josephine, as she opened a package of honey-roasted almonds.

"Here's a plastic bowl I borrowed from the dining room," Jo answered, handing her a dish. "I didn't think anyone would mind." The bowl went rolling across the room as it dropped out of Josephine's hands before Allison could grab it.

Allison retrieved it quickly and filled it with the nuts. "How are you doing these days, Jo?" she asked quietly, setting out some plastic wine glasses on the dresser.

Josephine gave Allison a puzzled look. "What do you mean?"

"What do you mean what do I mean? Honey, I've been

noticing things lately. You're holding onto walls when you walk, and you're always finding an opportunity to sit down. That's not like you. I know you don't drink too much or take drugs," she laughed. "So what's up?"

Allison's question hung heavy in the air. Allison *would* be the one to confront her with the one question Josephine did not want to deal with.

"I don't *know* what's happening. I was hoping no one would notice. I think it's just that I'm handling too many things right now." Jo's throat hurt with the constriction of holding back her feelings.

"Jo, dear, I'm worried about you. Have you seen a doctor?"

Josephine saw the concern in Allison's eyes. She hated anyone worrying about her. "I don't know what's happening, damn it. I wish I did." Jo's voice was higher than she meant it to be and it quivered. "I just can't deal with this now. I haven't the time."

Allison gave her a who-are-you-kidding look.

"Actually, I did see a doctor and he said it was probably stress. He wanted me to see a psychiatrist."

"You? A shrink? Baloney!" exclaimed Allison. "You're the sanest person I know!"

Josephine hugged her. "Thanks, Allison. The doctor made me feel as if I were losing my mind. If *you* don't think I'm crazy, then I'm not. What I could use is a different doctor." *But if there is nothing wrong with my mind,* she wondered, *then what is going on with my body?*

There was a light tap at the door. "C'est moi."

"Entrez, Monique," called out Josephine. She turned quickly to Allison and said in a whisper, "Don't worry. I'll see another doctor as soon as I can. I'm sure it's nothing serious."

⊸•⊷

Felice pulled a jacket out of her tiny closet. "I can't tell you how glad I am that you've made these new friends, Mother. I knew that's all you needed."

You're trying too hard, Carol thought. *If you don't want anyone to tell you what to do with your life, why don't you lay off me?*

"Sorry I won't be able to join you and your group before dinner," Felice continued. "I have to discuss a case I'm working on with Abby."

Carol stared at her daughter. "Can't you escape from your practice for even one weekend, Felice?"

Felice didn't reply, and after a few silent seconds Carol said, "Okay, please yourself. I'm late and I'd better be going." She turned and walked out of Felice's room.

They were all there at Josephine's when Carol pushed open the door. Maevis and Annie were sprawled on the floor like two teenagers. Josephine was propped against the headboard of the bed, with Allison at her feet. Monique was curled up in a chair twirling a half-filled wine glass in her hand.

"What are we drinking?" Carol asked.

"I'm having a wonderful Sonoma merlot," Allison said. She got up and walked to the chest of drawers where there were two open bottles of wine and paper plates with snacks. "Or would you prefer a white?"

"White, please." Carol took the glass from Allison and picked up a handful of small pretzels. Nobody asked her about Felice and she made no explanation.

Carol liked these women. Annie and Maevis didn't take themselves too seriously. She'd known Monique for a few months, although not as well as she would have liked. Josephine was vivacious, interested in everything and everybody, although Carol suspected there were some problems brewing under the ever-present smile. And Allison. She seemed so compassionate. Carol found a place on the bed next to Josephine.

"I'll drink wine, but I don't eat junk food anymore," Maevis announced.

"I can skip the chips too, but I'm nuts for nuts," Annie said, helping herself to another handful of almonds.

Maevis laughed. "Speaking of nuts, did I ever tell you guys how I met my husband?" She winked at Annie, who had heard the story several times before.

"No, how?" Josephine encouraged her. "I'll bite."

"Well, Josephine, tell me first whether you believe in fate." Maevis tried to look earnest. "You see, I think Neal and I were meant to be together. Destiny. I'm sure it was more than just chance that I won him in a SCRABBLE® tournament." She paused for dramatic effect.

"A SCRABBLE® tournament?" Carol said. "I didn't know there was such a thing. I've heard of chess tournaments, but —"

"Yes," Maevis interrupted, "it's true. And now they even pay big money, as Vanna says, "Big money." Not as much as chess, but maybe someday. Anyhow, I used to be very good at the game. Don't laugh! I'm a fantastic speller, and I memorized a lot of weird words."

"So where was this, Maevis?" Josephine asked.

"In Oakland, ages ago. I was still living in Berkeley, and some of us went to the tournament. We were very serious players. We got together every week through FUB. Don't you remember the Free University of Berkeley? They had all sorts of oddball classes.

"So, I was really hot at this Oakland tournament..."

"I'll bet," Allison smirked.

Maevis ignored her and continued. "It was the final round. There were four of us left, and I was hoping I'd get to play Neal, who was a newcomer, an unknown. See, I knew the other two fellows. They were killers. It turned out I didn't play Neal, but somehow I ended up the winner of the whole thing anyway." Maevis took a sip of wine and beamed.

"So what happened with Neal?" Carol pressed.

"Oh, afterwards, a bunch of us went to a Chinese restaurant nearby and — would you believe — Neal tried to order in Chinese! See, he once lived with a Chinese family and had picked up a few words. Such a showoff! Then, the guy sitting next to Neal across the table from me, this guy pulls out a cigarette. Neal says loudly, 'You aren't going to light that up *here,* are you?' and when the guy answered in the affirmative, Neal gets up and moves to an empty seat at the other end of the table, as far away from the cigarette as it was possible to sit. He absolutely loathes smoking," Maevis explained.

"But here's the best part. Neal sits down next to a guy he thought was safe, see, who then says with a straight face, 'Yes, but I have bad breath,'" Maevis cackled. "I love that part! The guy really said that with a straight face. Well, anything's better than smoking to Neal, so he retorts, 'I'll take it.' And everyone at the table was hysterical."

"So, it was love at first sight?" Carol asked.

"Sure was," Maevis answered. "I'm a sucker for a guy who can take it when the joke's on him. At the end of the meal, I passed him my phone number and said, 'If you're ever in Berkeley, look me up and we'll play. Meaning play the word game. But we ended up playing a lot more than that." She winked.

"I'll bet," Allison smirked again.

"Oh no!" Josephine cried, shaking with laughter. "I've spilled my wine." Allison grabbed a few napkins and mopped the bedspread as best she could.

"Yes, three months later we were married," Maevis finished. "And that's how my life, such as it is now, began."

"Well, I've heard all kinds of how-I-met-my-husband stories, but that one takes the cake," Carol said. The room was hushed for a few moments, with only sounds of munching, sipping and sighing.

"Ladies," Monique then spoke up, "I don't usually talk about my late husband, but if you don't mind, I'd like to tell you how we met, Andrew and I."

"Monique, we'd love to hear how you met Andrew," Allison said.

"We're all ears," Josephine spoke for the rest of them, "aren't we?"

"I was eighteen years old and working in De Gaulle's government-in-exile in Algiers," Monique began. "I was just becoming aware of young men. My father would bring home

American and British soldiers to have dinner with us so our family could practice speaking English. At the end of November one of the regular guests asked if he could take me to a Thanksgiving party being given for the American military. My parents hesitated because a nice girl should not be seen walking in the streets with an American soldier, they'd always said. They believed that my reputation would immediately be jeopardized.

"However," Monique continued, "since they trusted this particular officer, they acquiesced."

"Yes, I remember the sailors in San Diego during the war years," Carol joined in. "They were only interested in getting laid — pardon my French!"

Blushing, Monique went on. "We arrived late at the party, and I was introduced to several GIs and their girlfriends. Then I witnessed the event that would change my life. It was a beer-drinking contest between two sergeants. One was the typical army man, the kind you see in the movies shouting orders to the enlisted men. The other was a young soldier trying to keep up with the big guy. How my heart went out to him! There he was drinking one beer while his opponent, towering over him, drank three glasses without even breathing hard. When it was over, the soldier I came with walked over to the defeated soldier and said, 'Tough luck, buddy.' Then he introduced him to me, and that's how I met my Andrew."

"Bravo!" Allison cheered.

"Andrew took me to a table covered with food such as I had not seen in years. We did not really suffer from hunger in Algiers, but pastries, ice cream and rich foods were absent from our diets.

The Jewish refugees from France lived mostly on citrus fruit and vegetables grown behind our homes in small gardens. Eggs and chickens were plentiful, but beef was out of the question. We did not drink milk or have butter for five years. Can you imagine? That night I literally gorged myself on sweets and ice cream while talking about everything and nothing with Andrew. I lost my natural shyness."

"And is that all you lost?" Annie asked innocently.

"Be quiet, you naughty thing," Maevis told her. "Let Monique finish."

"When I returned home, I was jubilant. I told my mother all about the evening and especially about the young GI whom I wanted her to meet very soon. Naturally, I did not mention the beer competition. When they finally met, Andrew charmed my mother, who did not speak English, by conversing with her in German."

"That's so romantic, Monique," said Carol.

"I find it amazing how Cupid arranges for us to meet," Allison commented.

"This is just like a girl's pajama party, and I feel like a kid again," Annie giggled. "And I've got a funny story about Stanley and me when we were first married."

"Let's hear it," Josephine settled back against the pillows. "I can stand one more."

"When Stanley got his residency at Stanford Hospital and we moved to Palo Alto, I was very homesick. Stanley was aware of my loneliness, so he decided to buy me something special to keep me company. He brought it home after work one night and handed it to me with a big grin. I opened the bundle and shrieked when I saw this large rodent staring at me with its dark eyes. It had a black face and a white body. 'Stanley,' I screeched, 'why did you bring me this ugly rat? It's repulsive!'"

"A rat?" Maevis asked, her eyes wide.

"Not really, but I thought that's what it was. Stanley was disappointed at my reaction. 'Gee, I thought you'd appreciate some company,' he said. 'And it's not a rat, it's a guinea pig. A gentle and friendly pet.'"

"After a while, I grew to love the furry little creature. Our local grocery store gave me wilted lettuce and carrots to feed my Fluffy. I bought him a leash to match his complexion and a tiny bell to hang around his dainty neck. I became his devoted care-taker. I even took him to the park. One afternoon, I packed a picnic lunch for myself and some veggies for Fluffy. It started off as a very relaxing day, but after an hour I noticed peculiar behavior. Fluffy was desperately trying to find some cover from the afternoon sun. He had made his way under the blanket, but now he was barely moving. I panicked when I saw his limp body. Quickly, I gathered my belongings. I picked up the semi-dead fur ball and ran home in tears.

"When I reached the apartment complex, I ran up the stairs, unlocked our door and grabbed the phone. 'Stanley, come home, the guinea pig is dead!' I yelled into the mouthpiece. My whole body was trembling. I was choking with tears and trying to make myself understood. 'I've killed him,' I wailed.

"Stanley tried to calm me down over the phone. He gave me instructions. 'Fill the sink basin with cold water and immerse

Fluffy for five minutes,' Stanley, the doctor, prescribed.

"My hands were shaking as I held Fluffy in the cold water. My fingers began to lose feeling, while my upper body was drenched in sweat. I couldn't help thinking how hopeless it all was. How pathetic to see the wet creature expiring right before my eyes! 'It's all over for Fluffy and it's my fault,' was running through my head."

Annie paused for a moment and sipped her wine. The others waited expectantly. "Just then, I heard Stanley at the door fidgeting with the key. He ran to the sink where I was standing and took hold of Fluffy.

"'I've killed my sweet companion.' I couldn't stop crying.

"'It's only a guinea pig, Annie. Get a grip!' Stanley tried to reason with me. 'We can always buy another one at Woolworth's.' "

Just then a miracle happened. There was movement in Stanley's hands. The wet critter shook his body weakly, then more vigorously.

"'Get some greens for him and some champagne for us,' Stanley said to me triumphantly. 'Fluffy is alive and kicking!'"

Maevis was rolling on the floor with tears in her eyes. "You've never told me that story before, Annie. Did it really happen or are you making this up?"

Josephine glanced at the clock on the table beside the bed. "Hey, enough stories—true or not! It's time for dinner," she announced. "And, by the way, guess what I'm doing tomorrow?" She surveyed her five friends. Nobody offered a guess, so Josephine plunged ahead. "I'm going to have my first massage.

When I was looking over the herbal display earlier, I met the owner's son, and he recommended their massages."

"Massages are wonderful," Carol said. "I get one every month."

"But..." Josephine hesitated, "the only opening was with a mister Somebody or other."

"So?" Maevis asked, "What's wrong with that?"

"Well, I'm having trepidations and palpitations about a man massaging me, that's what," Josephine replied. "It's not something I'm used to."

"Don't be silly," Carol interjected. "My masseur is a man. He's terrific, and I feel perfectly safe with him."

"And, I must confess," Maevis emptied her glass saying wistfully, "I love the feel of a man's hands on my body."

Six

"I'm so glad to be here at the spa," chirped Annie, as she, Carol and Maevis left the dining room that evening after their meal, "even if I may have forgotten to turn off the stove before I left. You know, I was already on the freeway when I thought of it, but I was *not* going to turn back. Since I haven't received a call from the fire department, I guess Stanley must have noticed the flame before he went to bed and turned it off."

"I told you, Annie. What you need to do is stop babying your husband and boys so much and do the things *you* want to do," Maevis scolded. "Let Stan and your grown sons learn to fend for themselves."

"We all reach a point in our lives when we have to make decisions that are good for ourselves. It's just that some of us women take longer than others to reach that point," Carol added pensively.

"I've got my Neal trained to take care of the kids and give me lots of time to be a woman as well as a mommy. Why, you should see him get all three kids bathed and tucked into bed in less than an hour. He's a whiz!" Maevis boasted.

"Wait for us," Monique called out from behind. "What are

you gals gabbing about?" she asked, as she and Josephine hurried to catch up, with Allison trailing behind them.

"Annie was just telling us that even though she may have forgotten to turn off the stove before she left, she's not sorry she came away this weekend," Carol told them.

"Annie, you didn't walk out of the house and leave the range on, did you?" Allison joined up. "Well, as long as you didn't have your guinea pig sitting on it," she teased.

Monique spoke up. "You all know I'm a widow now, don't you? But I've met a new friend whom I just telephoned. Earl's his name," Monique reminded them. "He said he misses me, and I miss him, too. It's wonderful to know there is someone waiting when I get back to the city. I have a feeling this relationship is going to turn out to be something important for me."

"Monique, Neal and I came to the conclusion early on in our marriage that a little absence makes the heart grow fonder — and the sex better, if you know what I mean."

Allison stared at Maevis in disbelief. Did the woman have no modesty? Secretly though, Allison wished Brad would want her more when she returned, like he used to. But she was sure that her being away just made it easier for him to spend all his time on his electronics project. She noticed the rest of the women agreeing with Maevis, however, so she tucked her thoughts deeper inside herself.

They all strolled in the direction of the lounge where the evening activity, a journaling class, was to take place. No one had seen the room yet, and they were pleased with its cozy ambiance. Paneled in a light-colored wood, the lounge held four plump beige sofas set in a semicircle facing a large table. Fresh flowers were placed here and there, and at the back were game tables with padded chairs.

"Welcome ladies," a striking woman in a silk apricot pantsuit greeted them. "Please take one of these handouts explaining what I've planned for you this evening. Also, there are clipboards to lean on and pens to write with, because we all are going to write tonight. Make yourselves comfortable anywhere, and I'll explain more when the rest of the journal writers arrive."

Monique took a paper, clipboard and pen and headed for one of the sofas. Maevis and Annie plopped down together, and Maevis began moving the throw pillows around behind her back until she found the most comfortable arrangement for herself.

Carol murmured that she needed something more substantial to write on and headed for a game table behind a sofa. Josephine joined her. Allison glanced about and finally walked past Josephine and Carol and settled herself alone at the far table.

"What are we — pariahs?" Josephine called out to Allison. "Come sit here." But her friend just shrugged and stayed where she was.

Carol whispered to Josephine, "I probably should have asked before I signed up, but what exactly is this 'journaling'?"

"Don't worry," Josephine answered. "She will probably suggest a topic and then you just let your thoughts flow freely on paper. Stream of consciousness it's called. I learned about it in my freshman English class."

A dozen or more guests had entered the lounge. Words of welcome were passed about as the newcomers settled in, a few women opting for a cross-legged position on the floor. When the room was almost full, the leader began.

"Welcome again. I'm Louise and I'm going to be your guide tonight. We are all here at this beautiful spa to cleanse our bodies, and the first exercise we'll do here is going to help you cleanse your souls as well.

"Journaling has become very popular lately as a way of releasing your innermost thoughts, things that you never get to tell even your best friends. So far, you may have pampered your body with healthy food or massage, but tonight we will address our emotions. If you've never done journaling before, be assured that anything you write is okay, and everything will be only for your eyes, unless you choose to share your writing with the rest of us. The handout each of you was given explains a few additional pointers." She stopped and smiled broadly, looking slowly around the room to make eye contact with each of them. "Are we ready to begin?"

Louise pressed a button on her tape recorder and soft music filled the room. "My suggested topic for tonight is: 'Something I've Never Told Anyone.' Remember, it's therapeutic to rid yourself of the excess baggage you've been carrying around for years. Let your thoughts flow backward, back in time without self-editing. Take a few minutes to feel. You may begin at any time."

Allison, alone at the back of the room, felt a tightening in her stomach. She wasn't ready to confront her troubling issues with Brad, and she didn't know what she was going to write until the pen met the paper.

But Mom, we ate the last cookie in the house for dinner yesterday, she wrote.

Allison stared at the sentence in front of her and then studied the heads of the other women absorbed in writing. The cookie incident had been the absolute lowest point in her entire life. Had enough time passed so she could write about it? *Oh, what the hell,* she thought. *Perhaps this is as good a time as any to let go of my shame. I won't sign my name.*

She continued writing as if the story were about another person, not herself. She used the third person pronoun *she* instead of *I,* but the names of Allison's children were emblazoned on her heart and she could not change that.

Allison continued to write. *She hunched over to hide from her children the tears that would not stop coming. She tried hard to summon the courage to provide the care they required. But her own pain at Alex's abrupt departure was so great that she remained sitting, almost catatonic, oblivious to the needs of her young brood. Instead, she stared, hypnotized, at the gold links of the fireplace screen, remembering how she and Alex had purchased the fire screen together.*

It was an impressive custom-made fireplace screen. She and Alex had ordered it for the latest of their new homes, each thick gold link fitting neatly into the next to make a magnificent cascade. Now, literally, the links of her very life were coming apart. Whose hands would now link to hers? Where was her own link to life?

As she wrote, Allison recalled the suffering of those days right after Alex left. She wrote and it did make her feel better to get it out.

Her older son said, 'Mom, it's 7:30. We're all hungry. Please come and make dinner.' With tremendous effort she turned slightly in the direction of the boy and, casting about for anything so he would go away, she said, 'Why don't you and the kids just eat cookies tonight?' It was then that the boy had blurted out the sentence that woke her up. 'But, Mom, we ate the last cookie in the house for dinner yesterday.' How could I have sunk so low? Allison wrote in the first person, switching pronouns at last.

My children had always been perfectly fed and bathed and dressed, my home nearly immaculate. After all, that's what a good wife was supposed to do, wasn't she? But I knew inside myself that I hadn't been a good wife or Alex wouldn't have left. It was that one cookie sentence that brought me to my senses at last. I hugged all three of my children at once, gathering them into the circle of my arms and murmuring comforting words into their sweet necks. It was in that moment that I knew I had to face the fact that Alex wasn't ever coming home again, no matter how many tears I shed. And furthermore, I realized that I was going to be the only one to take care of myself and the kids.

First, I had to feed us. And since the little money Alex had given me as household allowance had run out, I had to find someone to borrow more from. I helped the children put on jackets against the chill February night and shepherded them into the car. My first two neighbors weren't home, but the third gave me more than enough money for the fast-food restaurant. He also gave me the name of a divorce attorney. Calling that attorney was the first important thing I had done on my own since I had met Alex when I was a teenager. And that was the day I stopped calling myself 'Allie.'

Allison put her pen down. She heard the leader ask if there were any volunteers who wanted to read what they had written. Monique raised her hand and said, "I'll read if you don't mind."

"Thank you, that would be terrific," Louise answered.

Monique rose and began reading. "Before the Second World

War, when we still lived in Paris, we had an apartment with two entrances, like all 'bon bourgeois', which my parents prided themselves on being. One entrance was for the family and friends, the other for the housemaids, solicitors and delivery men.

"One morning Maman had to go somewhere and I remained alone in the flat. I loved to be alone, because then I could do as I pleased — read, listen to the radio, even daydream. You see, my parents, mostly my mother, came from the old school that believed you had to be occupied every minute of the day. Reading was a luxury which Maman believed should not take up too much of one's time.

"She told me that a delivery boy was going to ring the bell at the back entrance and bring us the meat she had ordered by phone. I was eleven years old, but already quite developed physically. Small-boned and short, the shape of my budding breasts was visible through my blouse.

"In the middle of the morning, the bell rang and I went to the back door to let the delivery boy bring in the items. To my surprise, I saw a man at the door, not a boy, as I had expected. This would not have mattered, of course, but then something happened.

"The man took a few steps into the kitchen, put the package on the table, and turning to me he said, touching my breast with a quick, stroking manner, *'Comme c'est jolie ça!'*" Monique looked up from her paper. "That means, 'How pretty it is,'" she explained, her face reddening.

"Young as I was, I knew he had overstepped the bounds of propriety. Indignant at his vulgar gesture, I straightened up to my full height, looked him in the eye and pointed at the door. 'Sortez!'

I ordered. Still smiling, he left. After I had closed the door I realized that I had not given him the tip which Maman had left on the table for that purpose.

"When my mother returned, I just told her that I had forgotten to give the man the coin, and she did not pursue the question. The secret remained with me forever." Monique looked around. "Until now," she added. "Thank you for the opportunity to tell about this." She quickly sat down.

"Thank *you,* Monique," Louise answered. "I'm sure that your story stirs up memories for a lot of us. Does anyone have anything to add?" she asked the group.

"I, too, was touched like that by a man," someone called out. "And I never told anyone about it either."

"I told," someone else commented, "but no one believed me. I had to avoid him for years." The room buzzed with women acknowledging similar uninvited sexual encounters when they were young. Then Louise asked for another reader, and Carol volunteered.

"Here's what I wrote," Carol started. "On a wintery Friday night, when it was nearly six o'clock and black outside, I was alone in the women's shelter where I work as a volunteer. I was trying to finish some filing and tidy up before I went home. I had no plans for the evening. I would just be alone again; so I was in no rush to get home. I was hoping the rain would ease by the time I was ready to leave.

"There was a tentative knock on the outside door. I listened and heard it a second time. I opened the door to see a teenage girl standing outside. Her straight brown hair dripped onto her pale face and hunched shoulders. She wore a long, shapeless dress. She licked her lips. 'I think I need help,' she said in a shaky voice.

"I pulled her inside and closed the door. 'You're soaked to the skin. You need to get out of those wet clothes. We have some dry things here in the closet.' I handed the girl a sweater, a pair of jeans, underpants and socks. 'Get out of those wet things, and then we'll talk. You can dry your hair with paper towels in the restroom, the first door to the left.'

"I sat on the sofa in the reception room wondering what I could possibly do. I was only a volunteer. And what could the problem be? What was this youngster running away from? When she returned in a few minutes, I found out.

"She sat at the far end of the sofa. 'I've... I've never worn jeans or a sweater before. I've never...' She stopped talking and tears spilled down her cheeks. I moved closer to her and took her hand.

"'I'm Carol Montgomery,' I said. 'What's your name?'

"'Margaret.'

"'Tell me, Margaret, what are you doing out alone on such a night?'

"'I...I ran away.' She cried as she spoke. 'I couldn't help it. I can't take it anymore.'

"'Who did you run away from? Your mother and father?' She nodded.

"'Don't you think they are worried about you?'

"Again she nodded without speaking. The tears were large drops on her cheeks. 'Did they hurt you?' I asked tentatively.

"She lifted a fist to her mouth and bit it. 'My mother and father are crazy,' she whispered. 'They make me wear those awful clothes, anything else is sinful. They tell me if I even think of disobeying them, I will go to hell.' Her young voice cracked. 'I don't want to go to hell! I want to be a good daughter, but I want to have friends... I don't want to look like a freak.'

"'Why can't you have friends?' I asked.

"'Didn't you see me before? Look at me!' she cried. I recalled her appearance a few minutes ago when she'd arrived, with stringy hair hanging almost to her waist, her dull, high-necked dress and heavy black oxfords. 'Everybody at school thinks my family and me are weird. I can only wear those awful clothes. I can't wear makeup to school like the other girls. I can't even listen to music or go to a movie or watch TV or have a Coke like the other kids. That's all sinful and evil according to my parents. The work of the devil, they say. I have to collect my two little brothers and come right home after school. We can't even go to my grandparents for Christmas, because they have a party with music and singing.'

"My heart ached for this troubled girl. I was just a volunteer, not in a position to make a decision or take any action, and I didn't know what to do. So, I tried to try to reach one of the social workers from the agency. The first number gave me no answer. The second was a recording. The girl got up from the sofa and came to the desk. She twisted her hands and bit her lips.

"'Mrs. Montgomery, could you call my grandmother in Sunnyvale, please? I want to go to her, but I don't have enough bus money. She'll come and get me, I know she will.'

"I hesitated. I would be aiding and abetting a runaway. But how could I send this child home against her will?

"'How old are you, Margaret?' I asked.

"'Sixteen.'

I was surprised. I would have guessed fourteen.

"'It's okay for me to stay with my grandmother overnight, isn't it? My parents weren't home when I left. They were at a church meeting. We could say I was going to call them as soon as I got to my grandmother's.'

"Margaret gave me the phone number and fortunately her grandmother was at home. 'I'll be there in twenty minutes,' she said, when I explained about her granddaughter.

Carol looked into the audience. "That's all I had time to write. I've never told this to anyone because I'm not sure if what I did that night was legal. But the end of the story is that her grandmother petitioned the court for custody. In the courtroom Margaret's mother condemned and cursed Margaret's grandmother — her own mother — and even yelled at the judge. But Margaret, who desperately wanted to live with her grandmother, calmly stated her wishes and she swayed the court.

"Margaret and her grandmother called me a month later to thank me and let me know how things were going. Her grandmother bought her new clothes. She gave her a small allowance and Margaret bought her first lipstick and had her hair cut and styled. She got herself a part-time job after school in a frozen yogurt store and was making friends in her new school. They are very grateful, Dottie and Margaret, and still call me occasionally to keep in touch.

"When I think back to that night, I feel I made the right decision. I helped a lost young person find a new life and have a chance to be herself."

There were murmurs of approval when Carol finished. "Are you still working at the shelter?" one woman asked.

"Yes, I am," Carol answered. "I hope to continue indefinitely. I've found that it's very meaningful to me."

At the back of the room, Allison stumbled to her feet. She needed to get out of there. It was bad enough she had dredged up all those painful memories. She could *never* share them with anyone else, not even Jo. She hurried out of the lounge, ignoring her friends' quizzical looks as she ran. Maevis also saw Allison leaving, and she noticed a sheet of paper lying on the table where Allison had sat. Later, when the workshop was finished, Maevis would amble over and put the paper into her backpack.

Allison ran across the pool area, dim on this moonless night, and sought the solitude of her room. The dark cabin was a sanctuary. Shaking, she undressed, crawled into bed and under the covers, turned on the electric blanket. The journal writing session had been more disturbing than she had imagined. She'd known she wasn't ready to confront her problems with Brad and had thought it would be safer to write about the long-ago time when Alex left. Was she ever wrong!

Allison stretched her legs all the way to the end of the bed and spread her arms across the queen-sized mattress. *Just for tonight I don't have to please anyone, I don't have to take care of anyone, I don't have to have anyone in bed with me. I don't... I don't...* She stopped herself. *What is it I don't have to do? What is it I really don't want to do?*

From deep inside she knew the answer. Reluctantly she acknowledged that she *must* think through her issues with Brad. She knew the Brad problem was the true reason she had signed up for this weekend away from home. She mustn't waste time thinking about Alex. She had to make some very hard decisions about herself and Brad.

For the hundredth time she told herself she was creating a mountain out of a molehill, that she'd had one messed-up marriage, so why was she even considering ending another? Brad had been so good to her and the kids; she shouldn't rock the boat.

This time the clichés didn't soothe her or fill the void inside. For the past few months she had felt as if her tears were always pressing and crowding just behind her eyelids, waiting to overflow if she ever let her guard down. Now, here in this tiny room, alone at last, she was finally facing why she was so sad all the time. Now, she let herself cry.

Yes, things between herself and Brad had been great for a while. After the pain of their divorces, they had come together eagerly, like two halves of a broken cup. Their lives had been full — filled with activities for the five kids, her teaching and of course Brad's inventing. They'd had fun together, lots of fun, and she had been grateful that she was a married lady again, and not just Alex's ex-wife.

From the beginning they had been a very child-oriented family. Brad couldn't have been a better help. Since he worked mostly at home at that time too, tinkering in the garage or with his computer, he had been happy to help care for any child who was sick and couldn't go to school. He had willingly pitched in taking the kids to their after-school activities. Best of all, he was always there to comfort her when she'd had an especially hard day.

It was a system that seemed to work for all of them. Each was doing what they did best with Allison happily at the hub of all the spokes. But then, a few months ago, just as the youngest was getting ready to graduate from high school and making plans to go off to UCLA, Brad was approached by some venture capitalists who gave him a bundle to develop a working proto-type of his latest invention. In this harried time of Kevin's senior year, Brad had gone and rented a small building, hired some people, and was constantly involved in trying to get the business off the ground. Since their marriage, it had been Allison, Brad and the children. A plus B plus C. Now the children were scattered, and Brad was in love with a project that she didn't even understand. Both of Allison's building blocks, the children and Brad, disappeared at the same time.

Is this what the empty nest syndrome was all about? The children's absence seemed to sharpen the fact that she and Brad really had so little else in common. She wondered how she had never realized it. She loved to read and he loved to roam; she loved bridge and he loved boats; he invented new things and she wanted old things fixed. Now she was in an unaccustomedly quiet house, correcting papers by herself and trying to push her thoughts and feelings aside. When Brad did sit down next to her, they couldn't seem to find anything to talk about, and she felt her whole existence going down the drain.

Sometimes she felt like a large piece of plate glass about to splinter into a hundred jagged pieces. But the guilty thoughts were the worst of it. She couldn't help wondering if she *had* married Brad just to have a live-in father for her children. Had she married Brad for all the wrong reasons? Had the last ten years been just a charade, a play — and now did she want to ring down the curtain and go home? Home to where? To whom? To Brad? To Alex?

"Oh, Brad. Oh, Alex," Allison moaned, not knowing whom she was mourning, as she shivered alone in the bed.

Seven

Josephine was used to getting by with very little sleep. Early Saturday morning she was at the deserted pool just a half hour after the sun had come up. *How can anyone just walk into the pool?* Josephine used to wonder. *It's such torture when the water travels up, slowly freezing every cell along the way. It's a coward's way.* She liked *her* way better. With a graceful, powerful push, Josephine would dive off the side of the pool and arc into the water. Fingers would break the water, followed by head tucked into chest, straight legs locked together and toes pointed. The shock of the water was exhilarating. She would then begin a long swim through the pool to the other end, one breath for the entire trip. It was so quiet in the water. It was like dreaming.

But things had changed for Jo. The coward's way of getting into the pool was now hers. Josephine's last dive two weeks ago at Sam's pool-party had been a disaster. She had taken her mark to dive in from the side of the pool, but for the first time in her life a dive went awry. She'd heard the slap and felt the sting as her thighs hit the water. Her toenails had scraped the edge; her legs had not responded to the push off. A big belly flop!

Now Josephine kept her thoughts away from the hurt she

was feeling and pushed them down, far down, to that place which enabled her to hide from herself. It was there that she kept the knowledge that others were noticing she was sitting down whenever she could and dropping things she never dropped before. *How could Allison's questions have surprised me? What is happening to me, and how much more is there to come? What else is going to fail me? Damn!*

With this inkling of her limitations, Josephine walked into the water and pushed off from the shallow bottom into a dead man's float. Gliding face down into the deep end, she noticed something small and shiny at the bottom of the pool. *What could that be? Will my legs have enough strength to get me to the bottom to see what it is? Can I do this? And how much am I willing to gamble on this attempt?*

Josephine dived down with all her strength and went as far as she could, then came up for air. Not far enough. Again she went under, pulling strongly with her arms and shoulders. She came very close, but as she reached out to touch whatever it was, she realized she had to hurry back up for air. Fast. She'd gotten close to the bottom, but not close enough.

Josephine was determined to get the shiny object. But she was not diving just to get it. She was diving to prove something to the only one who needed proof — herself. Once again she went down. With powerful arm strokes she came close, but her legs were not helping. Her hand touched the bottom of the pool next to it, and then her fingers closed on the very small object. *Yes!* She shot back up and broke the water at the top gasping for air. *I've got it!*

She opened her fingers a tiny bit, trying to keep her chin

above water at the same time, and glimpsed a small piece of jewelry in her fist. A few thin golden links, a broken chain, lay on her palm. She stared at it as if she were seeing a long-lost friend. *I'm going to keep this forever. Anytime I think I can't do something, I'll look at it and remember that I can do it — I can!* Her fingers closed firmly around the treasure.

"Hello," a friendly voice sang out in greeting. "I thought that was you, Josephine. What are you doing up so early? You're supposed to be on vacation here."

Jo did a slow breast stroke over to the side of the pool and pulled off her swim cap. She ran her fingers through her hair, fluffing blonde curls. "It looks to me like you, Mr. Jack, are permanently on vacation here." She couldn't help but notice his tanned legs beneath the cut-offs that he was wearing with a colorful Hawaiian shirt.

"I found a sample of something new in the herb department that's supposed to be great for fatigue, Josephine. It might work for you. Interested?"

"I might be," Josephine flirted.

"It's called ginseng. It's an old Chinese herb. Want me to get it for you? I have some in my office."

"Okay, I might try it if you think it's good, Jack. Hand me that towel, please. I'll change and meet you in the office."

Jack had some tea brewing when Josephine arrived. She sat slowly and asked, "So what was the 'long story' you didn't have time to tell me before?"

Jack looked at her a little blankly.

"You know — about starting college and what you studied and all that."

"Are you sure you want to hear about it? It is a long story," Jack teased.

"I've got plenty of time to listen," Josephine smiled.

"Well, after my dad died, I missed him a lot and had a hard time concentrating and fitting in at college. My classes seemed trivial, so I'd leave school from time to time to help Mom at the spa on the big weekends or holidays. I liked doing that, but Mom always insisted I go back to school.

"Finally, I got my degree and I took the money I'd earned and went off to do my own thing. I went to Mexico and to the Latin American countries. When I got to Peru, I loved the place and especially enjoyed the people. I dressed like they did, and for one year I even sounded like they did; at least they said my Spanish was that good.

"But what appeared to be the simple life was not so simple. There were many dues to pay. The most extensive game was respect — whom to respect and when. It was fascinating, but not easy to learn.

"I got involved with some Indians in Peru — particularly a young widow. When I eventually realized that her village would never accept me, we said our goodbyes, and I came back.

"Mom's spa still appealed to me when I returned. It was all informal relationships, except for the small crew, and I was sick of hierarchy, pecking order and giving respect due. I settled into a life of helping at the spa and taking a few classes at the college, just for myself.

"Gradually, I drifted toward classes in healing and holistic medicine, including herbs. I steered the spa in the direction of natural, organic food from our garden, put herbal supplements up for sale in the lobby, and added classes in yoga and Tai Chi.

"Little by little, I got more involved here. I decided to take some business classes too, so I could understand more about that end of running a spa. I hired almost every one of the crew in place, and they began to come to me for solutions to their problems or mediation of their quarrels. Mother has lately been relying on me more and more, and I found that I enjoy our success.

"So there you have it. I promised you it was a long story," he said.

"And that's why you're so knowledgeable about vitamins and herbs. Thanks for sharing the lowdown with me." Before Jack had a chance to probe Josephine for her life story, she quickly asked, "Now about ginseng, tell me more. How long has it been around?"

"Ginseng is a common Chinese herb. It's been around for thousands of years. It removes mental and bodily fatigue while boosting energy."

"No side effects?"

"Nope."

"Then I do want to try it," Josephine said enthusiastically.

⎯⎯◆⎯⎯

Focus, girl, focus. You can do this. Maevis had done many more difficult bits of acting in her younger days and was undaunted. She inhaled, adjusted her backpack over one bare shoulder, and hurried over to the pool. She headed for Allison who was lying on a lounge chair with a book on her lap.

Maevis' imagination leaped and tugged like a puppy on a leash. *Cool it,* she reminded herself. *Don't jump to any conclusions. You've got to have more information than just the childrens' names on that paper of Allison's. Remember, your goal is to see some photos.*

Maevis plopped her backpack down on the white plastic strips of the chaise next to Allison. She stretched audibly. "Oooohhh, this is such a gorgeous day, isn't it?" She sat down. "I love it here, don't you Allison?"

At the mention of her name, Allison peeked out from under the wide-brimmed hat covering her face, but didn't say anything. Her book fell onto the ground, but she made no move to retrieve it.

Maevis reached into her bag and pulled out a tube, unscrewed the cap and began rubbing suntan lotion on her legs. A pungent aroma of coconut oil permeated the air. "I can't imagine *what* my husband and kids are up to today. He was a sweetheart to give me time off — for good behavior, I guess," Maevis laughed. There was no response. She leaned over and picked up Allison's book.

"Oh, *Ship Fever.* I just *love* Andrea Barrett. Are these short stories good?" Still no answer. "My husband will probably take the kids to the park to throw the baseball around. He's such a jock. I just hope he remembers to brush Chloe's hair afterward. It gets so tangled otherwise."

Maevis reached into her bag again and pulled out a wallet. "Look," she said, thrusting a dog-eared photo toward Allison. "Here's the little imp. Chloe's only six, but does she ever have her daddy wrapped around her finger! And doesn't she look like Margaret O'Brien in 'Little Women'? You remember that old black and white movie, don't you, Allison?"

Allison removed her hat and looked up. She saw a dimpled little girl with brown pigtails staring out from the picture. "Yes, she's very cute," was all Allison said. She lay back with her eyes closed.

"Do you have any photos of your kids, Allison?" Maevis asked. She held her breath and waited. There was no response from Allison.

Then slowly, Allison reached for her straw bag. She put her hand inside, brought out a small photo album and pulled off the ribbon. "These are my three when they were kids," Allison pointed to the open book, handing it to Maevis. "The other two are my husband's from a previous marriage. Of course, they're all grown now."

Allison looked directly into Maevis' sunglasses. "Seen enough?" she asked in a harsh voice. She grabbed the album back and pushed it into her purse. "Now will you *please*... let... me... rest!" She enunciated the last three words sharply.

"Sure, sure," Maevis nodded earnestly. She'd needed only a glance to confirm what she had suspected after skimming the paper Allison left behind at the journal session. Maevis was sure now that the tallest boy in the photo was Alex's son, Mark, the one she had met a long time ago in Berkeley.

"But," Maevis couldn't stop herself, "I know him, your son." She was pointing at nothing, to the place where the photo had been before Allison yanked it away.

Allison looked horrified. She sat up. "How would *you* know my son?" she asked, incredulous, her voice rising. The two women stared speechlessly at one another.

"You're Alex Evans' wife, aren't you?" Maevis finally uttered. Her words seemed to float forever in the morning air, an ugly accusation.

Allison heard herself murmur, "Yes," and then she quickly retracted it. "No, no, I'm Brad Boyce's wife! I'm *Brad's* wife!"

But it was too late. The damage had been done. In that ominous split second, both women fully realized something that neither of them had wanted to know. They had both loved the same man.

⟫◆⟪

"Wait, Allison, wait!" Maevis shouted as Allison ran off. "I only saw your boy once. Alex was living with Trudy then. Allison!" But Allison was already too far away and heard none of this.

What did I do? Maevis picked up her backpack and lotion. *That look on Allison's face... she's really freaked out! I must find Josephine. Jo will be able to help her.*

Maevis ran to Josephine's cabin. "Please be here, be here," she chanted as she banged on the door, but there was no response. *Allison has it all wrong! I had absolutely nothing to do with Alex's leaving her. I didn't even meet him until two years later, when he was already with Trudy.*

"Josephine, where are you? Where the hell are you?" Maevis searched the main lobby. Everyone knew Josephine, but no one had seen her that morning. Maevis tried to keep her own breathing slow and steady as she'd learned at childbirth class and as she did while jogging. *Establish a pattern,* she reminded herself as she began running down the path. *Inhale two three, exhale two three. Slow and steady. I've got to find Josephine, she has to go to Allison. The woman needs help. What have I done?*

Just then Maevis saw Annie in red shorts coming towards her. "Thank goodness — Annie, Annie!" Maevis slowed down, so relieved to see her pal that tears came to her eyes. Here was someone to explain *her* side to. Dear Annie.

Annie ran up to Maevis. "What's wrong?"

Maevis clung to Annie. "Annie, I'm unjustly accused, and I've done nothing, I swear."

"What are you talking about? Who's accusing you of what?"

"Remember when I told you about my early days in Berkeley, before we met? Remember that time after skating when we went out for a glass of wine, and we talked for hours?"

"Yeah, I remember. So?"

"Remember the guy I told you about — my old man, Alex? The one I was living with? The one I still think about?"

"Yes. What, are you seeing him again?"

"No, nothing like that. It's just that I was talking to Allison a few minutes ago, and it turns out that Alex was her first husband. He left her and their three kids years ago in L.A. When I told her I knew him in Berkeley, she got up and ran away. She must think I broke up her marriage, but it's not true. I didn't meet him until later. She thinks I stole her husband from her. She hates me!"

"Calm down, Maevis. She'll understand once you explain it to her."

"No, she won't even listen. She ran away. I've got to find Josephine. Jo's the only one who can get through to Allison, but I can't find her. Oh, where is she? Have you seen her, Annie?"

Annie put her arms around her friend. "Shhhh, Maevis, settle down. Why do you care anyway whether Allison believes you or not? What's the difference? *You* know what really happened, and *I* believe you."

"Annie, that was the one thing I made certain never to do, come between two people or break up a couple. I never went after a guy who was involved with someone else. When I was in high school and college, I wouldn't even go to the movies with my girlfriends and their fellas. 'Three's a crowd,' I'd say. Everyone would laugh at me, but I never went without my own date, and I never flirted with my girlfriends' guys either."

"Maevis, I'll come with you to look for Josephine. Maybe she's over there in the hot tub on the ridge. Have you looked there yet? C'mon."

"Oh, Annie, I'm so glad you're here. Thank God you came this weekend." The worry left Maevis' eyes. "I don't know what I'd do without you, you're so sensible and... and... grounded!"

<hr />

Allison knew Alex had hooked up with some little hippie at Berkeley, but to meet her in the flesh and to realize it was that Maevis person she already disliked, was the ultimate injury to her already vulnerable ego.

Allison hastily made her way back to her cabin after the confrontation with Maevis at the pool. A housekeeper wheeling her laundry cart blocked the pathway. She turned and said to Allison, *"Que pasa, Señora?* You okay, Ma'am?"

"I'm not feeling well." Allison squeezed past her. "Is there any way I can have lunch — something hot — brought to my room?"

"I'll ask Miss Ursula if I can bring you something. You like soup?"

Inside, Allison slumped against the door. This was the only haven she had now. She curled up in the armchair and lifted her feet to the ottoman. She was plagued with questions about Maevis and Alex. She wondered if Maevis had ever heard stories about her from Alex. Did Maevis know how she had begged Alex for months to come back? How she had cajoled him into balancing her checkbook each time he picked up the kids, just to have him in the house a little longer? Had Alex and Maevis made little jokes together when the man Allison was seeing went back to his wife?

Allison was so ashamed. She couldn't believe that Alex had abandoned his family for some little tramp. She feared that at this very moment Maevis might be whispering all her dirty tales to the other women here at the spa. How could she possibly face anyone again?

Eight

Carol had come prepared for yoga. She put on tights, a leotard and a baggy sweatshirt. Heading for the exercise room, she saw Monique with a towel over one arm.

"Hi, Monique," she called out. "Are you taking the class?"

Monique turned around. "Yes, I am. Is that where you're going?"

Carol nodded and they walked into the room together, settling themselves on their floormats. "What are your plans for later?" Carol asked.

"Nothing in particular."

"Well, let's do nothing in particular together then," Carol suggested.

For the next hour, they pushed and stretched and maneuvered their limbs into positions of which neither believed she was capable. At the end of class, they replaced their mats and left.

"That was so relaxing, wasn't it?" Monique sighed.

"Not exactly the word I would have chosen." Carol laughed. "But I'm glad I did it. Now I can feel virtuous for the remainder of the day. Where do you want to go?"

"How about up there on the knoll? We can sit under that

huge live oak. Did you know that some of those trees are hundreds of years old?"

"No, I didn't. You've certainly learned a lot from the Sierra Club hikes."

Monique spread her towel on the lawn and sat with her knees drawn up to her chest, her hands closed around them. Carol lay down on her side, her face shaded by the tree.

"I could stay here for the rest of the afternoon and do nothing, absolutely nothing," she told Monique. "Do you still go to the dances at that widow's group? I've only gotten up the nerve to go by myself twice on Saturday evenings when I was completely bored and could think of nothing else to do.

Monique said. "I haven't gone back. Don't you remember? I met someone, the man I danced with all evening."

"I sure do remember. That nice fellow with the green tie — what was his name?"

"Earl. Earl Leonard."

Carol laughed. "You still remember his last name?"

"Oh, yes. I know quite a lot about him. We are seeing each other, as a matter of fact."

Carol sat up. "Really?"

"Yes," Monique explained. "We've been dating steadily. We have so much in common, you see. We both love to go out on hikes and go bike riding together. He's very comfortable to be with and we talk easily. He's a quiet, gentle man and he makes me feel like a loved woman. I haven't felt that way with anyone since my husband died."

"How long has your husband been gone?" Carol asked.

"Six years," Monique replied. "Andrew had cancer, and he

went very quickly. There wasn't enough time for me to accept the reality that he would be gone forever."

"I've been a widow for only three years, but sometimes it's hard for me to remember what it was like to have Robert." Carol paused. "He went to his office one morning, and then in the afternoon... in the afternoon I got a call from the hospital that he was dead." Her voice broke.

"You never get over the loss, the emptiness," Monique said softly. "I like Earl very much and I know he loves me, but it will never be the same as it was with Andrew. I was only nineteen when I fell in love with Andrew."

"I'm not looking to meet another man. I don't know if I want to risk losing someone I love again."

" Carol, I'm glad we're talking about this. I want to confide something. Earl has mentioned us living together."

"That sounds great — if you want to, that is."

"I'm torn. Now that my daughter is married, I live alone. I want to be with Earl, but I wasn't brought up to live with someone out of wedlock." Monique looked at Carol intently. "At our age it doesn't matter, though, does it?"

"The youngsters do it. And at our age we don't have to be concerned about getting pregnant, do we?" They both laughed.

"But I've been thinking about what Earl suggested," Monique continued, "My daughter and her husband like him a lot. They get along so well, and Earl adores my granddaughter. It shouldn't really matter if we don't have a legal piece of paper. Earl has told me that he wants to be with me only, to spend the rest of our lives together. I believe that he's sincere. I know he's not suddenly going to change his mind and pick up and leave. Confidentially, if I get married again, I'll lose Andrew's pension and my health insurance. And then there is Earl's sister who is a spinster and a bit worried. But even if we don't get married, we can still live together. That's okay, isn't it?"

"It's more than okay if you find a man who is willing to make a commitment and who knows what it means to be faithful." Carol moved closer to Monique and put an arm around her shoulder. "If you love and believe in one another, at this point in life you don't have to worry about pleasing other people. Do what is right for you in your heart. Take what happiness you can find."

Monique nodded her head and they sat in silence for a few moments.

Then Carol spoke again. "I met someone I cared for very much a year and a half after Robert died. This man was retired and had more time to spend with me than my husband ever had. Robert was a successful stockbroker. He worked evenings and weekends; I didn't see him all that much.

"I guess this new man turned my head. He took me to the theater, the opera, the best restaurants. I even went on a cruise with him. Then suddenly he wasn't available any more." Carol stopped. "It turned out he was married. His wife had been in Chicago for six months taking care of her mother, who was seriously ill. I was just a fill-in while she was gone. That's one reason why I'm not looking to meet a man anymore."

"I can understand your feeling like that. He could have been one of those men who always cheated on his wife, and it could have just gone on without either you or she knowing how dishonest he was. It's good to be out of a relationship like that."

"Yes, I know. I've gotten over him. Now, I have my women

friends to go out with to movies, shows, dinner. And, of course, there's my volunteer work at the shelter. It's very fulfilling."

"Yes, that was an interesting story you wrote last night about that poor young girl. I admire you for what you did." Monique looked approvingly at Carol. Then she looked at her watch. "Do you think we should head back? It's almost time for lunch."

"Of course. I wouldn't miss it. The spa's mineral drink and those prune-sweetened nonfat cookies for dessert. Let's go!"

<hr>

There was no light under Allison's door. Josephine knocked anyway. Perhaps Allison was taking an afternoon nap." Allison! Allison, are you there?" Josephine knocked again. "Helloooo...," she crooned. Josephine had spent most of the morning in Jack's office, and Allison hadn't been at lunch. Was she lost on a trail? Jo wondered if she should notify someone. *Oh, yeah, Allison would love that. A fuss being made over her. Allison's most unfavorite thing.*

No fuss, Josephine decided. She opened the small hiking bag into which she had tumbled the contents of her purse. She found a folded sheet of paper. It was the program with Allison's name on it from the luncheon. *This is the right stuff,* Josephine thought.

"LET ME KNOW WHAT YOU'RE UP TO, OR I WILL ORGANIZE A SEARCH PARTY!" she printed, and she signed it "RANGER JO." She slipped the note under the wooden door knocker carved like a California stellar jay. Josephine smiled. Her own door knocker was a red cardinal. Sam, her boss, would never have stayed in her cabin — he was a U.C. Berkeley graduate. The

Golden Bears were fierce rivals of the Stanford Cardinals. Silly football fanatics!

Josephine departed with a sigh. *Where the hell is Allison? I'll check back here after my massage, if I'm not a complete limp noodle.*

She headed for the massage room. It was next to the small gym, now empty, which was used for yoga and dance classes. Josephine stopped at the closed door. She could hear an exotic, soft plucking of the strings of a high-pitched instrument coming from within. Her hand was damp and slipped off the door knob as she tried to turn it. *Why am I so nervous about this massage?* she asked herself. A jasmine scent escaped from under the door when it was opened from the inside. Josephine looked up — directly into Jack's smiling face.

"What are you doing here?" she gasped.

He took her hand and drew her into the room. "I'm your masseur."

"Why didn't you tell me?" She did not pull her hand away.

"You seem like the type of person who can handle the unexpected. And anyway, my name was there on the sign-up sheet."

"That was you?"

"Still is me," Jack smiled. As if he knew Josephine would want the facts and start asking questions, he began explaining. "Remember what I told you about helping to take care of my dad? Well, I used to watch his therapists give him massages, and I started doing it for him, too. He loved them, and the body work helped him a lot. Later on I got my massage certificate."

He motioned to a curtained area off to the right. "There's a gown in here you can change into."

"Oh," Josephine said, "this sweat suit is very loose. I'll just take off my shoes."

"If you take off your socks, I can do reflexology on your feet. Most people find that especially relaxing. Don't worry, Josephine. I've been doing this for many years. I'm adept at scalp and facial massage, also."

Josephine stepped on the stool, and then slowly moved herself onto the table. She took off her shoes and socks, and Jack put them aside neatly. He plugged in an artificial waterfall that began making soothing bubbly noises.

"Turn over onto your stomach and put your face here," Jack instructed, pointing out the headrest at the top section of the table.

"These sheets are warm," Josephine noted. "That's nice." She positioned her face into the hollow area padded with clean, white cloth. As he started working on her neck and shoulders, Josephine began to relax. There was caring in his touch; his hands felt warm and alive. The fact that he was a male was there, but it wasn't intrusive. Or was it? He was so good. He worked carefully and explained to her what he was doing as he went along. She was vaguely conscious of the music behind his voice. He lifted her top and put his hands underneath on her back. After a momentary sucking in of her breath, she forced herself to unclench as Jack continued the massage. After a few more minutes, Josephine was able to zone out.

Jack gradually moved up to the back of her head. No one had ever done that. His strong fingers gently worked their way through her hair. She knew his face was very close and she couldn't dream or drift away as she had when he was massaging her back. He was somehow too near now. She could feel his breath behind her neck.

This was the most intimate of all. She thought she felt his lips. No, that wasn't possible. What had she felt? It was something that barely touched her, tenderly. Was it a continuation of the massage? Was it her imagination? Was she dreaming awake?

Josephine was completely relaxed, so relaxed. *This is the kind of feeling I want to keep,* she thought. *I feel like the world is happy and in perspective, and my legs hardly hurt at all.*

After spending the afternoon holed up in her room, ignoring Jo's repeated knocking at the door, sometimes letting the relief of sleep wash over her, Allison knew that if she didn't show up for dinner, things would be worse. Then everyone would have a real heyday hissing about the fact that the enticing Maevis had stolen Allison's first husband. With renewed determination, Allison brushed her teeth and hair, washed her face, applied fresh make-up and started off for the dining room.

There she saw Josephine, Maevis and Annie seated together, laughing. Josephine, whose back was to the door, didn't notice Allison enter the dining room. In a corner, Carol and Monique were sitting alone. *Those are just the two I need tonight, two women who have lost their husbands,* Allison reasoned. True to form, when they saw Allison standing at the entrance to the room, Carol and Monique motioned her over and politely asked the server to set another place at the small table.

Each tried to get Allison into some light conversation. Monique talked about the yoga class they had attended. Carol mentioned the lovely spot on the grass where she and Monique had spent an hour talking after yoga. But Allison was still disconnected and was hardly able to respond. The dessert was delayed in the kitchen. No one passes up dessert at a spa, so they sat sipping their tea.

Over her third cup, Monique asked Allison softly, "Is there anything troubling you? Do you want to talk about something?" The way she spoke signaled to Allison that these women were the perfect pair to trust.

She cleared her throat and haltingly told them how Maevis had been badgering her at the pool that morning, and how she had discovered that Maevis had been her ex-husband's lover in Berkeley.

They murmured sympathetically as she told her story. Then Monique said, "But you certainly have grown a lot since your divorce. Look at you now. You're beautiful, remarried, have five lovely children and a whole list of accomplishments."

Carol looked at Allison intently and said, "Consider the fact that he probably left Maevis also, didn't he? I don't see what you should be ashamed about. He doesn't seem more than a self-absorbed bastard to me."

"Yes, maybe he did you a favor by leaving," Monique ventured. "You appeared so self-assured to all of us at the luncheon where you told your Jonas story. Why, I never could have spoken in front of all those people."

Allison smiled a little for the first time that day. "Thanks, you two," she said. "I really needed a couple of friends to talk to, and you've both been dolls. I hope we can see each other when we get back to the city."

"We'd love to," Monique said, giving Allison's hand a gentle squeeze.

"That's a great idea," Carol agreed. "We'll exchange phone numbers."

Dessert finally came, a luscious fruit parfait. When they'd finished and got up to leave, Allison turned to look for Josephine, but she was nowhere in sight.

"Let's go to the lobby and see what the others are planning for the rest of the evening," Monique suggested.

Carol and Monique were one thing, but Allison knew she could not face Maevis. "I'd better start my packing for the return trip," Allison said hastily and turned away.

"C'mon, Allison," Carol called after her. "How long is it going to take to throw everything into your overnight bag?" But Allison paid no heed and continued on her way, head lowered.

She didn't like walking past the pool and along the dark path alone. She quickened her steps. At the cabin, she had difficulty fitting the key into the slot and getting the door open. She tried again. *Oh, I can't seem to do anything right anymore. I can't even get into my own room.* When the door finally unlocked, Allison felt the total silence of the dark room envelope her. She stood and wondered what to do next. *I'll pack,* she decided.

Flipping on the radio, she carefully began to fold her clothes. She heard the full, rich chords of Chopin's "Polonaise in A-Flat Major." She hadn't heard that piece of music in ages. Someone had put words to it years ago and it had been "their" song, hers and Alex's. The words came flowing back.. "...'til the end of time...'til the rivers overflow...'til the end of time." Each chord was like another blow to her aching heart. She felt as though a dagger were plunging into her, again and again, for each of her abandonments — Alex's leaving, Brad's detachment, the kids going off.

'Til the end of time,' what a joke! And the tears rolled down her cheeks with the pain she had been holding back all day and the days before this one. She'd never be able to sleep tonight. Through the blur of her tears she fumbled in her purse for the bottle of pills.

⸺⬦⬦⸺

Carol and Monique found Maevis, Annie and Josephine in the lobby, where many people had congregated.

"So what are we doing tonight?" Annie was asking.

"There's going to be a lecture on colors. You know, which colors are best for your complexion and age."

"Oh, that's old stuff, Monique," Maevis snorted. "Let's do something exciting!"

"What happened to Allison?" Josephine asked. "I haven't seen her all day. I knocked on her door after lunch, but there was no answer."

Maevis looked up with a guilty expression, wondering if she should say something, but she heard Carol tell Josephine, "Allison had dinner with me and Monique. We invited her to join us for one of the activities tonight, but she said she wasn't up to it and went to her room to pack."

"To pack? Now?" Josephine exclaimed in disbelief. "Something's wrong. I wonder if maybe I should go to her."

Carol and Monique didn't appear worried and joined the others talking about evening plans.

"How about if we take off and go for a ride somewhere?" Annie suggested.

"Drive around here at night, Annie?" Carol shook her head.

"The roads are terrible."

Annie insisted, "I'll do the driving. I'm a very good night driver."

"Well, if you're willing to drive, then it's okay by me," Maevis said.

"Sounds like fun to me, too," said Monique. "I'll go. What about you, Carol?"

"If everybody else is going, sure."

"Not me." Josephine bowed out. "I'm stopping by Allison's room to see how she's doing, and then, since I'm still so relaxed from that wonderful massage, I'll just float off to bed. See you girls at breakfast."

The others went out to the parking lot. The early evening sky was still light. A few eager stars were visible. Maevis got into the front passenger seat of Annie's little station wagon; Carol and Monique sat in the back. Annie put the car in reverse, stepped on the accelerator and backed out. "We're just in time for a spectacular sunset drive along the ocean," she told them. "They say the road from here down to Big Sur is really something."

"It's something all right," Carol said. "Take it slowly."

"Oh, don't worry," Annie scoffed. "I'm used to driving mountain roads. The boys took judo lessons from some man up in the Santa Cruz mountains, and I had to drive them there two or three times a week for months."

As they passed the Rio Road entrance to Highway 1, Monique alerted them to the white monastery on their left. "I think it was built in the seventeenth or eighteenth century. A couple I'm friendly with went to Mass there. It was open to the public, and they were thrilled to hear the exquisite singing of the cloistered nuns behind the screen. Someday we'll have to come back just to explore the grounds."

They passed the turnoff for Point Lobos State Reserve. "Have you ever been to Point Lobos?" Monique asked them. "There are some very nice hiking trails and little coves that you can walk down to near the water. And sea lions. The Spaniards called them sea wolves. That's what 'lobos' means in English—wolves."

"Monique, you are better than a tour guide," Maevis complimented her. They passed several deserted beaches. The sun was an orange globe hanging low over the Pacific. Broad amber streaks shimmered across the calm water.

The road began to turn. They passed a sign indicating the California Sea Otter Refuge. Now the two-lane road was winding, all curves.

"Look!" Monique exclaimed. "From here, the cliffs just drop off into the ocean. Isn't it exciting?"

Annie took a sharp turn a little too quickly.

"Hey, slow down, Annie!" Carol called from the back. "I'm glad you're sitting by the ocean side, Monique. These sheer drop-offs are a little too much for me."

"Omigod!" Maevis shouted. She unfastened her seat belt and swung around completely in her seat to face the inside of the car.

"Hook your seat belt, Maevis," Annie commanded. "We'll get a ticket if you ride unbelted."

"A ticket?" Maevis screeched. "Who's going to give me a ticket? What other idiots are driving this road?" She pressed one hand to her breast. "I can't help it, Annie. I've been on edge all day, and now, we're so close to the edge. Literally. One little slip, and we'll be off the road and into the ocean. I can't look."

"Then don't," Annie replied calmly. "I'm driving very care-fully. My eyes are on the center line. Everything's going to be fine."

Monique leaned forward and tapped Maevis on the shoul-der. "Do you want to change seats with me and move to the back? I don't mind sitting in the front."

"No, not now! There's nowhere to stop the car," Maevis cried.

"Close your eyes, Maevis," Carol told her. "Stay turned around just the way you are and close your eyes." Maevis did as she was told. Carol spoke to Annie. "I'm not particularly happy about this road, either. We should turn around and go back as soon as we safely can before it gets totally dark."

"Okay, I will. But I have my eyes on the road. There's nothing to worry about," Annie insisted.

"I don't think there's a place to pull over and turn around anyway until we come to Pfeiffer State Park," Monique said.

"Well, please do it as soon as we get there, Annie. Maevis is frightened, and I'm nervous, too. Just turn around as soon as you can."

The rest of the trip to the Big Sur turnoff was driven in silence with Annie concentrating on the highway and Maevis crouched in the front seat with her eyes closed. Carol was hugging the left side of the back seat, her eyes glued to the inland side of the road.

Monique commented every once in a while about the disap-pearing sun, the splendor of the ocean or a ship out on the hori-zon, but no one in the car was listening to her. She kept an eye out for the Bixby Bridge, telling them that Jack Kerouac had lived near it and had written about it. That drew no response, either. She mentioned the famous cliff-side restaurant perched along the route that she'd visited with Andrew in the sixties, but still no conversation ensued about the scenery on Highway 1.

When they had started back, Annie told Maevis, "You can open your eyes. We're on the other side of the road now."

"Are we heading back to the spa?" Maevis asked. She had turned around in her seat and was facing front, but her eyes were still closed. "I will be so relieved when we get off this road. In fact, I will probably relieve myself immediately," she laughed weakly.

"Hold onto it, Maevis. Would you like to detour into the village of Carmel for a margarita? You can use the restroom there," Annie suggested.

"That's a great idea," Carol said. "After this drive, I think we can all use a margarita."

<hr>

Josephine stopped at Allison's door. Her RANGER JO note was gone, so she figured that Allison had read it and was probably inside. But when Josephine knocked, there was still no answer. She knew Allison had had dinner with Carol and Monique, and she could hear Allison's radio playing music. *Oh, well. At least I know she's okay. I'll see her at breakfast.* "G'night Allison," she called out.

Back in her own room, Josephine lay on the bed enjoying the lingering feeling of dreaming awake. Everything had a surreal quality since the massage. Then she thought she heard a gentle tapping noise and opened her eyes. The drapes were still open, but now it was darker outside. *I must have fallen asleep,* she thought. The tapping was repeated. It wasn't the wind.

Someone is here.

Josephine got up and opened the door. It was Jack. Why wasn't she surprised?

"Okay to come in?" he asked.

"Too late to say no, isn't it?" she smiled. It seemed natural for him to be stepping through the doorway into her room. He was her mood of the evening. He sat on the one chair; Josephine sat on the bed. She moved her legs under her, and when they came out of her peignoir, she wrapped them again.

"So what's happening?" she asked him.

Jack's face was partially lit by the moonlight coming in through the window. He looked at her long and hard. "I think *we're* what's happening. I feel something between us. I don't know what it is. Do you feel it, too?"

"I felt very close to you when you were touching me during the massage," Jo answered. Jack came to the bed and sat down next to her. He leaned close and kissed her. *What a lovely way to spend Saturday night*, Jo thought. *I wish it would last forever.*

Nine

B reathe, Allison, breathe!" Annie pleaded. She put one hand under Allison's neck near the base of her skull and the other hand on Allison's forehead. Gently, she tipped Allison's head back until her chin pointed straight up, which would prevent her tongue from blocking the airway. Annie put her ear down near Allison's mouth for five seconds to check for respiration.

She could see Allison had a pulse, but she was barely breathing on her own. Annie pinched Allison's nose shut, sealed her mouth with her own and proceeded to fill Allison's lungs with four quick breaths. Annie removed her mouth to check Allison's breathing again. Allison's haunted eyes were at half mast.

"Snap out of it!" Annie yelled at the dead weight in her arms. "You've got to make it!" *Was there anything else she'd learned in CPR class? Had she forgotten something?* As Annie continued the mouth-to-mouth resuscitation, desperately trying to revive her friend, she heard a commotion. Women were waking up, gathering around the pool and shouting at one another.

"Hurry! Somebody get an ambulance!" she heard a voice scream.

"Monique called 911 just now," someone else shouted.

Holding tightly onto Allison's cold body, forcing air from her own lungs into Allison's lungs, Annie remembered Allison's strange behavior at the journal writing class Friday night, that she left early and disappeared. She remembered what Maevis had told her about the incident with Allison at the pool yesterday morning, how upset Allison had been, and then how no one had seen Allison for the rest of the day. Monique and Carol said that Allison ate dinner with them Saturday night, but that she'd gone to her room immediately afterwards.

Annie searched for an answer. Allison was one of the first women she had met when she'd arrived at the spa, and Annie felt they had hit it off right away. *How ironic! One minute she greeted me at the registration desk with a warm smile and a welcome hug, and the next minute I'm saying prayers over her helpless figure, drenched in chlorine, lying here on the poolside tile. What a terrible turn to this weekend!*

Annie leaned down again to listen for a breath and saw Allison's chest rise and fall ever so slightly. Then she heard the sirens of the ambulance in the distance. "Thank God," she sighed. Annie stared at Allison's face and softly spoke words of comfort into her ears. "Hang in there, Allison, it won't be long."

Annie looked up and saw Monique running with two paramedics in white jackets. The men set down a gurney. One attached an oxygen mask to Allison's face. They checked her blood pressure, pulse and started an IV in her arm. They carefully raised her sodden body onto the stretcher, covered her with a blanket and carried her into the emergency van.

"Will she be okay?" Annie called after them.

"I think so. You did great. You saved her life."

Annie saw Monique get into the ambulance, and then one of the men shut the doors. The sirens blasted and they drove off. Exhausted, Annie dropped into a lounge chair and said another silent prayer.

———

Felice awoke to the sound of many voices outside her room, which faced the patio area next to the pool. She wondered what was happening, but was too sleepy to get out of bed. The noises grew louder. Felice tried to convince herself she should at least get up and look, but all she could do was flex her legs and close her eyes again. A pounding on the door of her room was followed by her mother's voice.

"Felice — open the door!"

She rolled over and sat on the edge of the bed. She felt for her slippers with her feet. *Where the hell are they?*

"Felice, let me in. It's important!"

Barefoot, Felice shuffled to the door and held it open for Carol to enter. "What's the matter, Mother?"

"Allison was a client of yours, wasn't she?" Carol's words came quickly. Her voice was loud and high. "Didn't you tell me you handled her divorce?"

"So? What's urgent at this hour of the morning?" Felice hoped her mother was not making a big fuss over a little thing. Felice thought her mother did that a lot.

"They just found her face down in the pool."

"What! Allison?"

"Annie went out for an early morning walk and saw Allison in the pool."

"Is she dead?" Felice turned and grabbed the pants of the sweat suit she had worn the night before and pulled them on, stuffing her nightgown inside.

"I don't know. I don't think so. She may not have been in the water long. She must have been out when no one else was around and accidentally fallen in."

Felice pulled the top of the sweat suit over her head and found her slippers. "Maybe she didn't fall in."

Carol stared at her daughter. "How can you even think that, let alone say it?"

Felice rushed out of the room with Carol right behind her. An ambulance was parked on the patio. They pushed their way through the crowd.

"Her respiration's shallow, but she's beginning to breathe on her own," one of the paramedics was saying as he slid the stretcher into the van.

"What hospital are you taking her to?" someone asked him.

Carol felt a tug on her arm. She turned to see Maevis with disheveled hair and tears in her eyes, her face contorted in pain.

"Oh Carol, it's all my fault!" Maevis whimpered. "I didn't mean to do it. I would never hurt anyone." Maevis ran her fingers through her hair. "I would never hurt anyone," she repeated mechanically. "Oh, God, what have I done?"

Carol grabbed Maevis by one wrist. The wrists were supposed to be pressure points where you could calm someone by squeezing hard, and Maevis certainly looked and sounded as if she needed to be calmed. "Maevis, settle down and tell me what you're talking about." Carol applied a steady pressure with her thumbs. "What's all your fault?"

"Allison. Allison in the pool. It's my fault," Maevis moaned.

"Don't be ridiculous!" Carol exclaimed. "Allison fell into the pool. It was an accident. How could you possibly be to blame?"

"I drove her to it. I know I did." Maevis' words came in short spurts. "Maybe I killed her. It's all my fault."

Carol grabbed Maevis' other wrist and squeezed both of them as hard as she could. Then she heard the screech of the ambulance's tires as it pulled away from the swimming pool area. "Monique went in the ambulance," Carol heard someone say.

Carol took Maevis firmly by the arm and moved her away from the dispersing crowd. She guided Maevis into her own room, sat her down and continued to hold the distraught woman's hands. Maevis' breathing seemed a little less jagged.

"Now settle down and tell me what this is all about. Allison's going to be okay, I heard the medic say so." She squeezed Maevis' hands in reassurance. "What in heaven's name are you accusing yourself of?"

"Yesterday morning I just had to talk to her about some-thing," Maevis' words tumbled out rapidly. "I saw her alone by the pool," she rushed on. "Everything seemed too coincidental, see. I was sure that Allison's ex-husband was my old boyfriend Alex from Berkeley, the one I can't stop thinking about. I saw what Allison wrote at the journaling session and their names sounded so familiar, a story about three kids eating cookies. Then yesterday she showed me photos of her kids. Sure enough, I was right. They were *his* kids. I recognized the oldest. I was right!" Maevis sucked in a new breath.

"The boy had come to visit Alex in Berkeley, but it was before he and I started to live together. I swear, Carol. When I told Allison I recognized her son from Berkeley... you can't believe the reaction. She looked at me with such hatred. She wouldn't listen. She ran off. And now she's jumped in the pool. Oh, God, what have I done?"

"Stop it right now, Maevis! Do you hear me?" Carol shouted. "Don't *ever* say Allison jumped in the pool. We don't know what really happened."

"I didn't meet Alex until two years after he left her, honestly Carol. He had been living with Trudy when I met him. Everything was so free and hang loose in those days that we just got together after they broke up. Oh, I loved him so much."

"Stop it, Maevis, I'm not interested in the details," Carol spoke as if to a naughty child. "Allison was probably just out for an early morning walk and was too absorbed to watch where she was going. I'm sure there's an explanation."

"But it's my fault that she was so upset yesterday."

"I'm sorry, dear, but you must get hold of yourself," Carol said, and gently rubbed Maevis' back.

Then Maevis began to sob. She wrapped her hands around her upper arms and rocked back and forth, bawling loudly. Felice had followed her mother and Maevis into Carol's room. She had witnessed the emotional exchange silently up to now, but finally asked, "Can someone here please tell me what's going on? After all, I am an experienced attorney."

"I can handle this, Felice," Carol told her curtly. Felice stared at her mother for a moment and then went back to her own room to dress.

"Look, Maevis, I'm sure Allison was upset when she realized you had been one of Alex's girlfriends. But stop crying and hear me out. Number one, he is her ex-husband. She has been happily married to Brad for many years now. And two, a combination of *many* factors, not just one thing, pushes somebody over the edge. It's never only one thing, so this can't be all your fault. Now pull yourself together." She spoke firmly but soothingly.

"Do you really think so, Carol? Oh, thank you, thank you! I don't want Allison to hate me. I don't want anyone to hate me. I'd never hurt anyone on purpose. I've never gone with a man who had another woman. Alex was free when I hooked up with him. I've got to get Allison to believe that."

"I'm sure we'll be able to talk to her and explain everything when she's feeling better. We can visit her in the hospital or wait until she gets home." Carol rose and pulled Maevis to her feet. "Come. I'm not a runner like you, but how about a good brisk walk before breakfast? We'll talk to the others and see what's happening."

━━━◆◆◆━━━

Josephine watched the scene in anguish. It couldn't be! Someone in the pool? Someone being dragged out? Who was it? The gathering crowd made a circle around the figures on the ground. There was a lot of noise. Her legs felt weak and she groped for a chair. Josephine could not see above the heads of all the people clustered around the pool, but something was wrong. There was a pain in her gut, a knot. She felt ill, but she had to know what was happening. Jo got to her feet and started toward the edge of the crowd. Then her foot hit something and she stumbled. On the grass, unhurt, she decided to stay put so the help would be directed where it was needed. That was what she rationalized, fearing that trying to pick herself up would prove too much of a chore. Then strong arms lifted her to an upright position on the lawn. Jack!

"Thank you," she whispered. "I'm fine now."

Their gazes held for a long moment, then he moved away into the center of the circle and was lost there. When the ambulance arrived, Jack kept the crowd back, out of its way. Josephine could tell that someone had been pulled from the water. The person was covered by a blanket and had an oxygen mask over her face. *Short red hair? Oh, no!* Josephine could see Monique walking quickly over to the ambulance and climbing in.

Jack returned and helped her up and into a chair, his hands around her waist. "It's your friend Allison," he said, keeping one hand on her shoulder.

"Oh, no!" Jo cried. "Allison!" She tried to get up.

"Don't panic, Josephine. Stay here. She's alive, thanks to one of the other women. Someone pulled her out and revived her. They said she'll recover. But what happened to you?"

"My foot hit something and I fell. I'm okay now, really I am."

"You don't look okay. You look pretty shaken."

"Allison is one of my closest friends, Jack, I've got to go to her."

"She's getting good care right now, Josephine. The hospital is only ten minutes away and they have an excellent trauma team. They'll pull her through. Let's go inside. I'll get you some tea."

Seated in the lobby, Josephine gripped the arms of her chair. *My God, Allison, what could you have been thinking?* Jack returned with two cups of tea. Josephine took a few sips and put the cup down. "Jack, I've got to call Allison's husband. I've got to tell Brad. I need to get my address book from the cabin." He walked with her and waited while she made a phone call. He sat close to her on the bed.

"Brad said he's leaving immediately, but it's an hour and a half drive from San Jose," she told Jack. "He gave me her son's phone number. Mark lives in Monterey, and he'll be able to get to the hospital much sooner."

There was no answer at Mark's apartment. Josephine left a message on his recorder. "If you want," Jack offered, "I can take you to the hospital."

"That would be terrific. I'm really not capable of driving," Josephine admitted.

She stopped at the doorway, put her hand on Jack's arm and said softly, "You take good care of me, Jack." He leaned down and kissed her. She rested her head on his chest for a moment.

<hr />

When the medics carried Allison on the stretcher into the ambulance, Monique ran over and announced, "She is my dear friend and I am going with her to the hospital."

They didn't contradict her, but helped her climb into the vehicle, which moved quickly down the driveway.

Monique sat next to Allison and gently stroked her hand, murmuring, "All will be fine, Allison, don't worry. You're going to be well cared for in the hospital. You must have lost your balance and slipped into the pool. That could happen to anyone, you know." Monique could not bear to think of another, more painful reason for Allison being found unconscious in the pool. She pushed those thoughts away.

In the ambulance now, Monique was re-experiencing her husband's death, and the idea of losing her friend was more than she could bear. Monique remembered the image that had interrupted her sleep for so long after her husband's death from cancer. She'd arrived at the hospital early in the morning and had found him lying still and lifeless, with coagulated blood on the corner of his lips. No one had noticed that he had died during the night. She'd run to the nearest nurse, stunned with fear and shock. The nurse had held and comforted her, but Monique then realized the finality of life and knew she would never again hear Andrew's voice.

Allison's head throbbed with the incessant ringing. *Answer it! Answer it! Will someone please answer the phone?*

The ringing of the siren woke her from what must have been a very deep sleep. She was wet all over and tangled up in her blanket. For the moment, she couldn't seem to remember where the phone was. She couldn't even remember where she was. Just peal after peal of the ear-busting noise. Why wouldn't it stop?

Allison thought fuzzily of the other times the phone had awakened her, right after Alex left. It would summon her abruptly. She knew it would be Alex calling to say it was all a mistake and he was on his way home. Allison would jump awake to answer the phone, only to hear the grating dial tone. No Alex. Just a dream, a wish, a prayer, for the hundredth time.

"Answer it," she cried out. But the words didn't come out right. She opened her eyes, or thought she opened her eyes, but it was so black she still could not see. *This boat I'm in is rocking, rocking, and the phone is ringing. I'm cold all over and my stomach is doing loop-de-loops in the air.*

"Find it, someone. Stop that awful sound!" Brad usually answered the phone at night, but Brad wasn't here. *I'll have to find it myself.* She tried to reach out with her arms, but they were held tightly against her body. Allison tried to think of what might be happening. She was all tied up like a gift with a big red bow. Was she someone's present? She rolled her head to one side to try to muffle the ringing. Someone nearby moaned softly. Who was it? Could it be she moaning?

"Allison, you're going to be all right." A voice floated by. "You're on the way to the hospital. Monique is here with you. You're...going...to...be...all...right."

Why is Monique here? What's this on my face? A hard rubber cup. Why doesn't Monique take it off? My arms won't work. Maybe they're broken. I'd better have Brad look at them. Brad can fix anything.

When they got to the hospital, Allison was wheeled off, and Monique was left in the emergency waiting room.

After what seemed a long while, a nurse came over to Monique and said, "Your friend is out of danger. Her breathing is nearly normal, but they're going to be running some tests on her for the next few hours. You look tired. We have a cafeteria down the hall on the left. Why don't you go get yourself a cup of coffee and something to eat?"

Monique bought some tea and a muffin and went outside to sit in the sun. She found a bench, but she couldn't seem to warm up. Her mind hovered between Allison in a bed in this hospital and Andrew, gone from her forever.

A car horn sounded and Monique looked up. Carol was waving. "I'm going to park and I'll join you," she called.

"Good," Monique called back. Carol would be welcome company.

"I'm glad you're here with me," Monique told her friend a few minutes later. "I've been feeling sad. Not just about Allison. This is bringing back memories of when... memories of my Andrew," she finished, her voice catching.

"Yes, I know," Carol patted Monique's hand, silently. Then she rolled her eyes. "You just won't believe my daughter, Felice. She raised a big fuss when I told her I was coming here to the hospital. All she could think of was that I was wasting her whole day, that she'd have to wait for me to come back to the spa to take her home. Since I had insisted on driving us this weekend, she said I was responsible for getting her home on time. It's Sunday, for pity's sake!"

Monique always tried to see the best side of any situation. "Well, she's a professional woman, so she thinks her time is valuable, I guess."

"And more important than everyone else's." Carol looked annoyed. "Anyway, I tried to explain to her that I'd only be gone about an hour. I know they're not going to let me see Allison. I just had to come and make sure she's going to be okay, but Felice couldn't or wouldn't wait. She stormed off looking for someone else to give her a ride. I'm sure she'll find a colleague to take her home, if she can't wait for me to get back."

"Maybe I can get a ride back with you," Monique proposed. "I came with Josephine, but she may want to hang around here a bit longer. She and Allison are very close."

"Sure thing. I'd love to have you ride back with me, Monique."

"Maevis came with us also. Did you see her this morning?"

"Oh, yes," Carol shook her head sadly. "She was very upset. Some foolish nonsense that what happened to Allison was *her* fault. But she had calmed down a bit when I left. She was in Annie's good hands."

Ten

An old man. *Who is this coming into my room? A tall man with long white hair and a leathery face. Not someone from the hospital. Smiling like he knows me. Do I know anyone who looks like a mountain man? My mind isn't focusing yet. Dark brown eyes. Oh, my God! It's Alex!* Allison reached to pull up the top of her hospital gown, but her arms were still clamped to the sheets.

"I was crashing at Mark's pad when a message came in. I heard about you on the machine, so I left him a note and came right over to see if there was anything I could do to help. I told the nurse I'm your husband," he laughed. His voice sounded flat and sing-songy to Allison. "I hear you fell into a pool. You know, I always told you to take swimming lessons."

He told me and told me. Everything I did he told me to do differently. Did I really fall into the pool? I don't know what happened. I was in my room feeling blue... remembering Alex when we were together, and how much I loved him. And worrying that maybe Brad and I would never get back on the right track again. Now, here is Alex in the flesh, and I can hardly recognize him. He and Brad are the same age, but Alex looks much older. He's changed so much. Where is the dark, curly-haired boy full of confidence, with a jutting jaw and a great mind, the boy that I fell in love with? All the while I've been missing that boy so very much, but this man with boots and the fringed jacket isn't that boy.

"I'm glad I got to see you today. I'm leaving for the Far East just as soon as the crafts fair is over. Japan, Bali and Hong Kong. Have you ever been there?"

What in the world is the matter with this man? Here I am tied to a hospital bed, they just saved me from drowning, and he's asking me if I've ever been to Hong Kong.

"Yes. I was there — with you."

"Hah! It was so long ago, I forgot. Hong Kong is going to revert to China soon. You ought to go again before it changes."

Allison blinked, trying to wipe away the still-lingering cobwebs.

"Also, I want to talk to you about Mark. I don't like the woman he's with," Alex went on. "But maybe this is not the best time to go into it."

Allison said quietly, "I've been trying to call the nurse, but they have my arms pinned to the bed. Do you think you could ring for her? I need my pillow fixed."

"Let me move the pillow for you."

Alex leaned over Allison and jerked the pillow. Seeing the poor results, he leaned over her and tried again. The door to the room swung open, but with Alex looming above her, Allison couldn't see who was there. No one entered, and the door shut again.

"That's better," Alex announced, straightening up. "Look, I

need to run along now, but be sure to get in touch if there's anything I can do for you." His boots echoed as he hurried down the hall.

Get in touch if there's anything I can do for you, Allison mocked. *But where was he all those years I did need him? Where was he when Mark ran away overnight or Kevin needed the ear operation? And who was he with when Ellen asked me over and over again, 'Did Daddy really want a daughter?' 'Yes, Ellen dear,' I told her, 'your dad wanted a beautiful baby daughter just like you. He still loves you. It's only me he doesn't love anymore.'*

I feel so rotten. There's something I wanted to talk to some-one about, but I can't remember... Brad. Where's Brad? I need a hug right now. I need a hug from Brad.

———◈◈◈———

"This is a heck of a way to get attention!" Josephine kissed Allison's cheek. "Here's something I brought for you." She handed Allison a stuffed otter with a seashell on its chest. "It's an authentic souvenir of Monterey County. I found it in the gift shop." She tucked the brown critter next to Allison on the bed.

"Cute," Allison smiled weakly. "Chocolates would have been good, too."

"Hey, I'm lucky to be in here at all; I had to sweet-talk the nurse." Josephine laughed and decided to get right to the point. "So, what happened, Allison?"

"I don't know," Allison answered. "I felt groggy when I woke up that morning, so I went for a walk to clear my head. The next thing I knew, Annie was bending over and yelling at me. All those blurry faces around me, and the phone kept ringing and Monique was with me."

"Allison, I called Brad and he should be here soon. They said the tests look good. Your brain seems to be intact, no permanent damage there."

"Thanks, my good friend. They told me I'm going to be out of this place by tomorrow afternoon. I can hardly believe it," she whispered.

"That's wonderful, sweetie. Jack said there'd be no problem if I wanted to stay at the spa tonight, so I could take you home if Brad weren't reachable. But I did get to him."

Allison nodded. Her eyes closed.

I'll let her sleep, Josephine thought and left the room. In the east wing waiting room, she found Carol, Monique and Annie.

"Josephine!" Carol greeted her. "The nurses told us to stay out here, that Allison needed to rest. Did you see her? How is she doing?"

"Allison will be okay," she told them. "She's sleeping now, and her husband's on his way. She expects to be released tomorrow afternoon. I've decided to stay overnight, keep her company here and drive home behind Brad."

"I can take Monique home for you," Carol offered.

"And I'll take care of Maevis," Annie told her.

"Maevis? Where is she?" Josephine asked.

"Oh, I left her sitting in my car outside in the parking lot," Annie answered. "She wanted to come here, but then changed her mind. She's afraid Allison doesn't want to see her, so she wouldn't come in."

"That's ridiculous," Carol said.

Monique looked at her watch. "If Allison's sleeping, and going to be okay, I think we'd better go back to the spa and check out. I'm looking forward to getting home."

"Yes, so am I," Carol agreed. "This weekend feels quite over with. Let's get going. I can telephone here tomorrow morning for an update."

⇒◆⇐

Maevis had been sitting in Annie's Toyota in the hospital parking lot staring at the peeling dashboard. She was thinking that surely the engineers could have designed a dashboard that would withstand sunlight. They could have used some material that wouldn't disintegrate in a few years. After all, dashboards were meant to sit beneath the glass where the sun hit, weren't they? Those brilliant engineers in ivory towers in Detroit knew that much, didn't they? Maevis sat there pondering the stupidity of some people and the cowardice of others.

A shadow fell across the instrument panel. Maevis looked up and gasped. She was peering right into the face that had been inhabiting her dreams for over ten years, Alex! He was smiling at her from the other side of the windshield. Even without the Berkeley beard she knew him. With the long white hair she knew him. She'd know him anywhere. The dark piercing eyes hadn't changed a bit, and they had her trapped in the seat.

"Alex, omigod!" Maevis squirmed to fish out a used tissue from her backpack, stalling for time and composure, sneaking a look at him from the corner of her eye and a look at herself in the rear-view mirror.

There was that smile, those hypnotic eyes that had figured in her subconscious for so many years, in her daydreams and especially at night when she couldn't fall asleep. Even while she was making love with Neal, whom she surely adored, she would see Alex. His eyes. His smile. Maevis wiped her nose, threw down the tissue and unlocked the car door. She pushed it open, almost knocking him down in her haste.

"Whoa, baby!" he called out, just as he used to when she was moving too fast back at their pad in Berkeley.

"I can't believe it's you!" Maevis flung herself into his arms. They embraced and then she backed off, holding him at arm's length and taking a good look. "Your hair's gone all white!" she exclaimed, "but then you're probably grateful to have any hair at all," she teased.

"You got that right, babe," he grinned and squeezed her in an embrace again.

"But what are you doing here, Alex? I thought you moved to Oregon." Maevis hugged him back exuberantly. "I ran into your pal Glackman a few years ago, and he told me you'd moved north to Mendocino and then to Eugene."

"Yeah, that's right. I was just down here visiting my kids before I take off again, and a message came at Mark's pad that my ex-wife was at this hospital. She took a dump in the drink. How about you, Maevis baby? What are you doing here?"

"Oh, it's a long story. But, there's so much catching up we have to do."

"Well, let's find a cup of coffee and we can get started," he grinned.

"Yes, let's! Look, I came here with a friend, but I'll write her a note." Maevis fumbled in her purse, pulled out a pen and a scrap of paper on which she scribbled, then tucked the note under Annie's wiper. "There! Let's go. I can't believe it's you after all these years."

Maevis sat beside him as he drove — his old '56 pickup no less. She could tell it was the same one, the now faded dark green paint. She remembered when it had been fresh and new, an Earl Scheib $29.95 job. Alex had been so proud of this truck.

She noticed the muscles flexing beneath his soft suede jacket. He dressed just as before. He was still strong, slender and masculine all at the same time. Maevis felt weak just looking at him. He was wearing jeans and boots, as he always had in those earlier years. She saw a plaid checked lumberjack shirt rolled up in the space behind the seat.

—◆—

Later, Maevis swore to Annie that she hadn't intended to end up in a motel room with him. They'd started with coffee, but had opted for drinks afterward at the funky neighborhood bar Alex found about a mile from the hospital. Maevis couldn't take her eyes off him. They talked. They laughed. She smiled. He winked.

After the second White Russian, Maevis wanted Alex to touch her as he used to. She forgot about Neal. She forgot about Chloe and the twins. Alex rambled on but she was unable to concentrate on his words. She found herself thinking of him kissing her slowly up and down her body. She ordered another drink, and she wanted Alex to make love to her. He was still talking as he led her into a strange room.

And then she knew she'd had too much to drink. She thought of the headache she would have the next day. She hated those hangovers. How the hell was she going to function, to take care of the kids? The more Alex talked, the more he became a caricature of an old hippie. Maevis began to see a sixties leftover, a loser trying hard to appear a swinger.

She had moved on; he hadn't. She wanted to yell at him. *Been there, done that. This is the eighties now! I only go to crafts fairs for birthday presents. Nobody makes a living that way anymore. My husband Neal has a real job. He's an engineer. We're putting money away for the kids' education. I'm a mother now. And I have a husband who loves me. I have a life!*

He took off his jacket.

"Alex, wait." Maevis suddenly knew she no longer respected guys like Alex. Neal had a friend who went out with a different woman every month. 'He won't commit,' Neal would say. 'He can't accept responsibility. He's afraid of long-term relationships.' Maevis had heard all the jargon, and she couldn't stand the guy. 'He only dates young chicks because the older ones can see through him. He refuses to grow up,' she'd tell Neal.

Maevis began to feel anxious. And nauseated.

"Alex, I just realized... I should go home."

"What, babe?" He was playing with the buttons on her sweater and blowing on her neck. And talking.

"I've got to leave." Maevis hated feeling like a tease. She hated not being in control of herself — or her stomach. And she didn't want to need Alex any longer. "Oh shit," Maevis rubbed her brow.

"C'mon, babe, you don't want to leave now. Not now. It's like old times."

"No, it isn't. Things have changed, Alex. I've changed. I'm married now."

"Hey, I am too, babe. I took the plunge again, so what?"

"Look, I've got to get home."

He threw up his hands. "Do what you gotta do, babe."

"But I told my friend with the car to go on without me, and now I have no ride home, or back to the spa or to the hospital... I don't even know where the hell we are."

"You really want to leave? The room's paid for." Alex lay back on the bed.

Maevis was buckling her sandals. "Yes, I do. I can't believe nothing matters to you but yourself."

"Hey, if you want to go, nobody's forcing you to stay," he put on a casual smile. "You're not stranded, even if your friend has left. There's a bus stop right down the street."

Maevis' jaw dropped as she stared at Alex, disbelieving. He was still the same as he'd been in Berkeley. A selfish, self-centered bastard. Only she didn't know it then. She'd been too young to see through him. And so had Allison before her.

⇒•◦•⇐

"Brad, oh, Brad! I've been waiting for you. Where have you been?"

"I was here before, but... but I couldn't come in."

"Why couldn't you come in? Do you hate me for having to be dragged out of the pool?"

"Of course not." Brad took Allison's hand in his. "I'm worried sick over you. How are you feeling? Does anything hurt?"

"I'm weak and a little dizzy and a lot confused, but it's much better now that you're here. Why couldn't you come in before?"

"Well, I rushed down here as soon as Josephine called. I started into your room without knocking and... and I came in just as you and some guy were kissing."

"Kissing?" gulped Allison. She tried to recall what Brad might have witnessed. "We weren't kissing!" she exclaimed. "He was just leaning over to fix my pillow. You silly man, did you think...?"

"What was I to think? What was he doing here anyway? That was your ex, wasn't it? You two seemed pretty chummy."

"Oh, Brad, my darling. Yes, it was Alex. He was over at Mark's in Monterey and heard a message Jo left on the recorder. He took it upon himself to come over, and I hardly recognized him when he came in. I'm dizzy, Brad, but not that dizzy that I don't know I was waiting for you, not him. Please Brad, hold me."

Brad wrapped her in his arms. "Allison, honey, what happened?"

"I don't know what happened. I can't really remember about... about the pool. I just remember taking some sleeping pills the night before and ... But, no, don't interrupt — let me talk. I don't give a damn about Alex!" Allison rushed on. "He was just my high school fantasy, and I did spend a lot of time mourning the death of the marriage, just as you'd mourn any death, but it's you I want, you I feel close to, you I need."

Brad bent down and kissed the top of Allison's nose, then kissed her gently on the lips. "Allison, I know you've been unhappy lately..." he began.

"Brad, don't be silly. It's just the kids all leaving, and you being so involved in the new business. You're the one I have always counted on." Her speech slowed. "I *have* been sad lately, very sad. I can't deny it. We'll have to...to...." Allison's eyes closed and she fell asleep while Brad held her hand.

Eleven

"Neal, I simply must to talk to you." Maevis and her husband were preparing for bed the following weekend. She pulled her head and arms into the extra-long, extra-large T-shirt she liked to sleep in and climbed into bed. "There's something I need to get off my chest tonight."

Neal spit toothpaste into the sink. "I'll be happy to help you with anything that's on your chest, Maeve." He grinned at her.

"Be serious, Neal," Maevis frowned at him. "I've been upset about this all week. I don't feel right keeping things from you."

Neal wiped his mouth, came into the bedroom and got into bed. Maevis snuggled next to him, not giving him a chance to pick up the newspaper. When he hadn't seen the paper, particularly the sports section, Neal liked to scan the headlines before he 'hit the hay,' as he always said. Maevis would usually wait until bedtime, when the children were asleep, saving the thoughts she wanted to share with him. She hated to compete with the *San Jose Mercury News*.

"I'm tired, Maevis, and I have an early morning meeting. I hope this is going to be short. I'll give you my undivided attention for five minutes max."

Maevis had considered taking Neal to Barney's Pub for this confession, thinking a beer might mellow things a bit before she laid it on him. But Neal didn't like going to smoky places. He was more comfortable at home and didn't need a drink to relax. It was she who was tense and needed something, but it was too late now. *Just tell him*, she prompted herself.

"Neal," she charged ahead, the sooner to get it over with. "I want to tell you that, on the whole, I am extremely satisfied with our marriage and family life. You know I'm not shy about complaining if something isn't right. Well, everything's fine, a nine-and-a-half on a scale of one to ten. You know how I always like to leave room for improvement! You and the kids are my most cherished people. I definitely don't want to jeopardize our marriage or threaten the status quo."

"So what's up, Maeve? Bottom line."

"We need to talk. Our marriage is in danger."

"Uh oh. How so?" He rubbed the back of her neck. "How's our marriage threatened?"

"It's me. I did something last week, and I don't want you to be mad at me." She tightened her shoulders as he prodded and massaged with his thumbs.

"Did you run up the credit card?"

"You know I hate shopping."

"Is it the car?" Neal's fingers paused for a second.

"No, damn it!" Maevis leaned her head to the side. "Oh, that's a tight spot. That feels great!"

"Well? Spit it out, Maeve. I can take it."

"Okay. I ran into an old boyfriend," Maevis whispered.

"Oh yeah?" He pressed along both sides of the upper part of

Maevis' spine, one vertebra at a time. "That's all? There are a few old girlfriends of mine I'd like to run into."

Maevis drew a long breath and sank her face into the pillow, giving Neal more of her back to work on. "Stop kidding around, Neal," she mumbled. "It was my old flame from Berkeley. The one I was hung up on for years. Remember Sunday night when I came home really late from the Monterey spa?"

"The night you kept me awake until three? You should run into old boyfriends more often!"

"Oh, you! Mmmmmm, you have the best hands. So, you're not mad?" Maevis turned her head over to the other side and went on. "Well, it was the weirdest coincidence. It turns out that my old man in Berkeley was married before our life together to one of the women who went on the spa weekend. And I'm finally over him now, I'm sure of that. Thank goodness. But it was such an eery coincidence that I ran into him down there."

"Life's full of 'em, weird coincidences," Neal yawned. "But what was he doing at the spa, anyway? Taking a vacation?"

"Not really; it's complicated."

"Listen wifey, I think our marriage is strong enough to withstand a few ghosts from the past." Neal rearranged his pillow, leaned over and kissed his wife on the cheek. "Night, Maev, we'll talk more tomorrow."

The waves crashed against the rugged cliffs of Big Sur as Jack helped Josephine over the rocks and sand to a tiny beach cove below.

"Seals," said Jack pointing.

"They're sunbathing," answered Josephine. "And they're sea lions."

In a secluded spot, Jack spread out a blanket and they sat down together. Soon they had their arms around each other. Jack put his lips to Jo's hair and wondered aloud whether when they had children they would have her flaxen hair.

"I was blond as a child," he told her, "did you know that?"

"I saw pictures of a little blond boy on your dresser. I knew it was you."

She'd understood what he had been thinking. It was like that; they thought in harmony. He wanted her and she wanted him. It was simple, or so it seemed.

Josephine and Jack had become inseparable. This was not easy to accomplish due to their work schedules and the geographic distance between them. Somehow, they made time for each other because they wanted to. And funny, she thought, how the distance started to seem so much longer as they sought each other out more and more. They did not share their growing intimacy with others, but kept it for themselves as a private delicacy to be savored by them alone.

Allison grumbled that Jo was seldom home in the evenings any more. She said it had been their favorite time to chat and she missed it. Jack's mother would often eye his jeep as it left the spa, turning her inquisitive face toward the road as though she could guess his destination just by sniffing. She stopped short of asking him directly where he was going, preferring prudence to satisfying her curiosity. Heaven forbid she should appear nosy, Jack had told Josephine.

This beach cove was the best for some seaside kissing, she

thought. To Jack, the sand felt good and so did his sweet girl. He kissed her tenderly on her neck and shoulders. "Josephine, my bonny Jo."

"Yes, Jack."

"Let's get married."

Josephine put her arms around him and they kissed hard and long.

"Big step," she said.

"Yep," he answered, "but you're not surprised I asked, are you?"

"No, I guess not. Look! Here's a little hollowed out shell we can use." She wiggled her finger through it.

"I think we can do better than that," Jack said. He produced a purple velvet ring box.

"Jack — you've planned this!" Josephine accused him, laughing. And he kissed the tears away when the laughter ran its course.

<hr/>

Annie stared at the dirty dishes from the evening meal. They still hadn't been loaded into the dishwasher. *I don't know what's wrong with me. I don't give a damn about anything since returning from that retreat. Things are not the same. I'm different. Even my feelings towards Stanley have changed. I thought I loved him, but I'm not sure anymore. I'm not sure about anything.*

Annie felt as insignificant as the untouched plates sitting in the narrow sink. The mundane routine of scraping and rinsing them seemed so pointless now. It was getting late. Stanley was reading a medical journal, the boys were studying in their rooms, and she was having an anxiety attack. *They don't even notice. I'm drowning in my own kitchen, and there's no one to pull me out.*

Her hands were wet and clammy. Her fingers tingled, her neck dripped with perspiration and she was itchy all over. Time seemed to stand still. *I wonder if I'm having a panic attack or are these the symptoms of a nervous breakdown?* Annie's head was throbbing with pain. She felt her legs weaken and her knees buckle. She tried to grab the back of a chair, but was too dizzy to hold on. She collapsed onto the floor. She tried to call for help, but her voice was muffled.

Annie had been able to save Allison from drowning, but no one was coming to save her. Stretched out on the tile, Annie felt her heart racing. Flashbacks of the blaring siren and red flickering lights taunted her. *Hang in there, Allison. It won't be long. Hang in there.*

Annie opened her eyes to the beginning streaks of daylight. She was still on the kitchen floor and the dinner dishes were in the sink, unwashed. *Was I dreaming? Have I been here on the floor all night?* She picked herself up and headed for the bedroom. She was unsteady on her feet.

Stanley was sound asleep. *How can he sleep so peacefully while I'm in pain?* Annie wanted to shake him and scream. Instead, she undressed and slipped into bed very quietly so that she would not waken him. Her teeth were chattering. Normally, she'd curl up against him for warmth, but now she did not allow herself to snuggle.

She was awakened by a ring. Stanley was gone. Annie reached for the phone. "H... hello?"

"Hey, what's up?"

Maevis! I wonder if she'll detect that I'm falling apart, Annie worried. But she was glad of the human connection.

"I can't explain it, Maevis; all I know is that I'm changed. It's a little scary to wake up one morning and find yourself on the floor, a stranger in your own kitchen, a man you've lived with for over twenty-five years totally oblivious. My home life has become meaningless. It's in shambles."

"What do you mean you woke up on the floor?"

"I was staring at the dinner dishes in the sink, and then I got all jittery, like a panic attack, and I guess I collapsed on the floor. Maevis, I actually remained there all night. I woke up early in the morning and went to bed. And Stanley was sound asleep through it all and hadn't even missed me."

"Oh, Annie, you poor thing! You must be exhausted. How about getting together at the rink after lunch, or aren't you up to it?"

"I don't know. Why not? The kitchen floor, the skating rink... what's the diff?"

When they met later that afternoon, Maevis hugged her. "Annie, you're trembling. Are you sure you're okay?"

"No, I'm not sure. I don't know how to share this with my family, but I don't feel the same as I used to about being a dutiful homemaker and caretaker. Who's going to take care of *me*? When is it *my* turn? I'm really bummed that my family ignores my needs and... I've just got to do something more with my life. I've got to get out of the house more, find a new challenge besides preparing superb flaky apple piecrust and freshly baked French bread."

Her emotions were mixed. On the one hand, Annie didn't really want to create an upheaval, but on the other hand, she didn't want things to remain the same in her life. "I'm really tired of taking care of business as usual, Maevis," she continued.

"Now you're talking, Annie." Maevis swung her friend out

onto the wooden floor and took her arm.

"Ghostbusters" was booming through the speakers, and the colored glass pieces in the disco globe twirled, lighting up the ceiling in a magical way.

A soft smile formed on Annie's face as the two of them glided around the rink in time to the beat.

"You know, Maeve, I've always enjoyed the arts, but I never gave myself permission to be frivolous," Annie confessed.

"Frivolous? What the hell are you talking about, girl?" Maevis shouted above the music. "I know people who take the arts very seriously. What exactly are you after? Do you just want a new hobby, or do you want to make a major change in your life?"

"I want to find my passion and discover my gifts — if I have any," Annie said. "I've always loved working with my hands. Come to think of it, I have some old Chinese brushes stacked away in the garage. My neighbor gave them to me when his wife passed away. She was a real genius, and she let me watch her paint whenever I wanted to. Maybe it's time I took some art classes."

Only that morning Annie had been stretched out on the beige linoleum floor crying for help. Now, skating alongside her pal and chatting away, it was hard for Annie to believe she was the same person. She squeezed her friend's hand as they both rolled off the smooth wooden surface. "Thanks for being here for me, Maevis."

"You betcha." Maevis squeezed Annie's hand in return.

⚒

Brad brushed a stray lock of hair from Allison's forehead. They had been sitting together in silence at home on the couch, Allison pretending she was fully recovered. Their new understandings were almost too fragile for words. Each was enjoying the closeness of the moment. Brad's strong, sandpaper cheek comforted her as he pressed against her pale face.

Allison looked deeply into the eyes of her husband, this short, stocky man, and thought, *Thank God he believes that there's nothing between me and Alex anymore. Poor Brad. He's so good. I couldn't bear to hurt him.*

"Brad," said Allison dreamily. "I've been resting here thinking of so many things. Mostly about us and the kids. About how lucky we are with them. I look at other families and I am so grateful for ours."

"We tried hard, honey. But don't stress yourself talking so much."

"No, there is something important I want to say," Allison continued. "I just got an ep... an epi — a revelation—that it's an unusual adult child who doesn't resent his parents for something. Some long harbored grievance, painfully remembered by the child, that maybe the parent didn't even know about.

"What I'm trying to say is that all parents unwittingly bruise their children, perhaps by indifference, perhaps by suffocating actions or whatever. And, Brad, our kids had good reason to be bruised what with the divorces, our marriage and relocation."

"But they are turning out great," Brad protested.

"That's just what I mean," Allison added hastily. "You were a wonderful father to all the kids. Sure, you and I had our differences, and Alex helped my kids also, but in the end, it was you and I who raised five great adults-to-be. I want you to hear my thanks, Brad, my big thanks for helping soothe some of the bruises on our five."

"We did it together, honey. I have to admit it is a good parenting partnership, and the kids seem to have inherited good genes. They each scurried to the hospital as soon as they heard about you.

"But I want to talk about *you* now, not the kids," Brad went on. "I was wondering what you are going to tackle when you're up and about. I don't want you to go back to school right away, Allison. Take some time off. The school year's almost over anyway. But I mean afterwards."

"I can't wait to start taking care of the guy who is the best thing that ever happened to me. I think after all that has gone on in the past two weeks, I'm going to be quite content to stay home and just cook for you and read and watch TV together — for a while anyway." Allison spoke with mock bravado and a lump in her throat, pecking Brad on the cheek.

"Allison," Brad's voice was intense, "Allison, my love, is that what you really want to do? No, don't answer. Let me answer for you. This whole excitement has set me to thinking. In fact, I was jelling these ideas while you were at the spa."

Allison shivered, her face pinched as she realized how important this moment was. She tried again to interrupt whatever Brad was about to say.

"No, let me finish," Brad insisted, squeezing her gently, covering her mouth with his finger. "Honey, maybe I'm not as bright as you are, but I must have been blind and deaf not to see how unhappy you've been with me lately. Hear me out, Allison. I love you very much and I know you love me too, but right now we're in a difficult place in our lives."

Allison could hardly breathe. She had no idea what Brad

was going to say next, but evidently he had thought this out very carefully and there didn't seem to be any stopping him.

"Allison, I saw you at that luncheon. I've heard you practice your speeches a hundred times, but *that* time I saw you — really saw you. And you know what you looked like to me? A tall, self-confident woman with a great figure and marvelous auburn hair. A woman who could handle the attention and approval of the audience. Believe me, Allison, they did approve of you —you as a person — not only of the idea of helping the needy children. There wasn't a woman in the room who didn't admire the way you dressed and the intelligence with which you spoke, the way you walked and the... everything."

"But..."

"Allison, you're good at this, and now that our kids are grown, you're ready for a step-up, not a step-down. I know you love your second graders, but since we no longer have the major responsibility of our own kids, maybe you should look ahead to something new and more challenging. I have no idea what that will be, but I do know that you don't want to just stay home with a middle-aged man who is struggling with his own attempts to succeed."

Allison tried to protest, but tears of gratitude welled up in her eyes as Brad continued. "Honey, I swear you've grown a foot taller in the last few years. You used to slouch over when I first met you, and you wore all those gunny sacks that hid your beautiful breasts and sexy legs. Now that you've let your hair grow out and curl — why, honey, you're gorgeous!

"Allison, you're ready for a second blossoming, and I've been so involved with my own inventions that I've held you back.

Lovely lady, I'm the one with the empty nest syndrome. In a way," Brad continued in smooth golden tones, "women have a lifetime rehearsal for when the kids grow up and leave home. They have all kinds of volunteer groups, bridge games, petitions to sign, and they *talk* to other women. But men don't know anything except work and family.

"I'm the one who was lost, honey, and I took it out on you by spending more time at work than I should have and taking away another element of your support system. Why, for a few minutes there I almost believed you tried to deep six because I made you so unhappy."

Allison almost jumped out of his arms. "Brad, don't be silly! I'd never do that. We will work this out, I know we will."

Encircling her again, Brad explained, "I think I may have already worked it out. Remember all that time I spent puttering? Well, my mind finally started clicking again, and I think there is interest in marketing my prototype."

"What kind of prototype? What does it do? "

"None of that is important now. We'll see what happens. The main thing is that we both need to change, to improve our lives, not to sit and sulk. Both of us are energetic and have a lot of living to do yet. We have to be open to making something happen. We just have to remember that and support each other to get there, wherever *there* happens to be.

"This is probably one of the longest speeches of my life, but it's just a first. From now on, we're going to really try to talk and solve things together."

"Brad, it's nice what you said about my second blossoming, and that I should find — find a second career. Right now, I can't think of what that would be. I want to stay side-by-side with you, but later if something comes along, perhaps we will see a fit.

"Remember," she went on, "I grew up at a time when a wife was always at her husband's side. The women I knew didn't think of careers of their own. Now I see that the world has changed. Thankfully, women use their education and skills for something more than changing diapers and cleaning house. I think I might like something more, but right now isn't the time for me to make that generational leap."

Carol examined herself in the mirror, front and side views. The black pantsuit made her look almost slim. She'd lost quite a few pounds in the months since she returned from the spa, and she had pledged herself to lose fifteen more. She was watching what she ate, joined a health club where she bicycled and swam, and had gone roller skating several times with Annie and Maevis. That was helping pull off those extra pounds she had permitted to pile up. And the two younger women were so entertaining with their funny stories. They made her feel accepted and at ease, despite the age difference.

She had a makeover at a Nordstrom cosmetic counter, where the salesperson recommended smoke and cinnamon eye shadow. In the bathroom, Carol flipped her small mirror to the double magnifying side and started to apply the new eye make-up. With the soft brown color of her hair, she looked younger than she had in the three years since Robert died. She patted the side wave over her forehead into place. It was remarkable what a difference the right cut and color made.

Carol didn't see Monique as often as she used to. Monique was busy with Earl. Carol remembered how scared she'd been the first time she had gone to a dance with Monique. Carol had been driving and they had circled the parking lot outside the clubhouse, not finding an empty space.

"It must be very crowded," she'd told Monique. "I hate crowds. Maybe we should go home."

"Oh, if there are a lot of people, we're sure to have fun. Plenty of men to dance with," Monique had replied.

She's as excited as a teenager, Carol thought. Carol was certain no one was going to ask *her* to dance, and she ached to go home. But Monique would have none of such defeatism. She tapped Carol's arm. "Look, there's a car pulling out."

Carol inched into the parking space. She and Monique got out of the Mercedes and headed for the entrance.

"You know," Monique told Carol as they walked, "I was completely alone the first time I came to a dance here. But you can't sit home locked in your house. No one is going to come knocking on your door looking for you. So I always force myself to talk to people. I put on my best smile, go up to a group of people and say, 'Hi, I'm Monique, I'm new here,' or I even ask a man to dance. And I've discovered most people are relieved to have someone else make the first move."

"You're probably right," Carol answered. "And I'm most people. I'm terrified."

"Think of this, Carol. You have a car, you drive, you're financially independent. You can go anyplace and do anything you want. You have a lot to be thankful for."

"You're right, Monique. You have a wonderful, positive

outlook on life. That's what attracted me to you."

Carol remembered realizing that Monique's attitude was exactly what would attract a man to her, too. And Monique had met Earl that night.

The phone rang. Carol put down her lipstick and ran to get it before the recorder clicked on.

"Hello, Mother." It was Felice, and she plunged right into a lecture. "Don't tell me you're really going to sell the house."

"I didn't tell you. How did you find out?"

"Well, there *are* public records, you know," Felice replied sharply. "One of my real estate friends told me the house is listed on the market. It doesn't make sense right now—"

"It makes sense to me," Carol interrupted, "because I don't want to rattle around alone anymore in this house your father bought to entertain and impress his business contacts. It's too much work for me to keep up alone."

"I can't seem to get you to think sensibly these days."

"You mean you can't get me to do what *you* want. I don't need this place. I'd be better off buying a small condo for myself and investing the difference. You, of all people, should under- stand that. Anyway, I'm just putting out feelers to see if there is a market for this immense house. On the other hand, there is a possibility I may be able to get some help with the house that would allow me to stay. Then I'll just take it off the market."

Carol could picture Felice frowning with disapproval. "Okay, okay, Mom. Just be sure to keep me posted. I hardly see you anymore."

"That's because I'm busy. I've been taking your advice about getting involved in outside activities, and it's been fun. Thanks for telling me I should do that, dear," Carol said warmly, hoping it would soothe Felice to know she'd listened to her. "Of course I want to see you, too," Carol continued. "If you'd like to get to-gether — and I have a few surprises for you — why don't we have dinner one night this week? In a restaurant. I don't feel like fussing in the kitchen to cook a meal for only the two of us."

"Just a minute, I'll look at my calendar," Felice said. "How about Thursday? EMILE'S would be convenient. I'll be in court, so I could meet you at 6 o'clock. I know you like good seafood, and they even have parking."

On Thursday Carol fussed with her new hairstyle. Why hadn't she colored her hair before? It made her look ten years younger. She hadn't bought new clothes yet, because she still wanted to lose more weight. She'd put on the trim black pants hanging in her closet, the ones she hadn't been able to bring herself to give away, that now fit her. Her favorite lavender cashmere pullover, pearls and pearl studs completed her outfit.

She spoke to herself in the mirror. "I can't believe this is me. Maybe... maybe..."

Carol arrived at EMILE'S before Felice and decided, what the heck, she'd have a glass of Chardonnay. She was sipping her wine when Felice arrived, dressed for court in a gray-striped suit. Her broad-brimmed hat was a paler shade of gray.

At first Felice walked right past Carol, but then turned around. "Mom! You look great!" She touched Carol's reddish brown pageboy. "I like the color. It's very flattering."

"Thank you, dear," Carol said as she deliberately slipped off the stool and spun around.

"Hey! How much weight have you lost?" Felice asked

admiringly.

"Twelve pounds," Carol answered with obvious pleasure. "Enough to fit into these pants I've always loved. But I intend to lose more. Soon, I'll be as svelte as you."

Felice cracked a smile. "What made you decide to do this? I'm thrilled. You were beginning to look like an old, frumpy widow."

"Thanks for the left-handed compliment," Carol laughed. Now that she'd lost weight, she could accept Felice's criticisms without feeling put down.

When they were seated, Felice at first declined ordering wine, but then she relented. She lifted her glass and extended it toward her mother. They clicked glasses. "Here's to a celebration of my new young mother."

Carol glowed inwardly. "We need to do this more often," she said warmly. "But let me tell you what we've been concentrating on at the shelter recently. We helped a fortyish Asian woman who ran away from her brutal husband. He kept her almost as a slave, but luckily for her, he was incarcerated for something else. We're helping her learn to be independent and to take care of herself. It is so gratifying for me. I know I am doing something worthwhile."

Felice reached over and patted her mother's hand. "I love you, Mom. I always just wanted you to be the best you can be."

———◆◆◆———

Monique always enjoyed going to Earl's bachelor quarters in Menlo Park. Since he'd met her, he had repainted all the walls and bought new modern furniture for the living room. He said he wasn't going to bring her to an old dingy apartment. He'd even gotten a CD player and some romantic music.

Monique had the feeling she was doing something forbidden when they made love, and since no one knew about their intimacy, the secrecy added to the excitement. Now they were lying on his bed, holding hands. Monique wore only her slip, and Earl, modest Earl, his shorts and undershirt.

"I love being here with you, Earl. I forget all my worries and think I'm a girl again, doing something my parents wouldn't approve of. They were terribly strict and protective of me, you know. However, in spite of it all, I was quite adventurous when I was young."

"I bet you were. You still are now."

"Yes. Coming to your apartment the first time took a lot of courage," Monique told him, "but as a girl I did not always do as was expected."

"I could guess that."

"When I was dating my husband Andrew in Algiers, my mother would always tell me to bring him home instead of walking around the city with him. She was so worried about my reputation if I were seen with an American soldier.

"There was a nice beach near Algiers called Franco Beach. Some of my girlfriends and Andrew's buddies used to go there to swim and socialize. To get to the beach we took a bus, or, more often, we drove an amphibious car which belonged to Andrew's platoon. When they weren't using those seagoing vehicles, they let the men take them. It was very exciting for me, at nineteen, to be taken to the beach through town in those strange cars. I never told my parents. They would have been horrified. They thought we always took the bus."

"Did you really get into amphibious vehicles? I remember them so well. That's how we landed in North Africa in 1942."

"You did? Well, sometimes a friend of Andrew's would drive, and then we would be in the back of the car necking."

"What a bad girl you were!" teased Earl.

"We would have to park before we came to the beach and then walk through a very dark tunnel."

"Did you neck there, too?" Earl gently poked Monique in the ribs.

"Yes, of course," Monique giggled. "But everybody used the tunnel. It was the only way to reach the beach, so our privacy was limited.

"I never disclosed this part of the outings to my parents. I guess they trusted me with Andrew, whom they liked very much. Andrew was not much of a swimmer, though. He was proud of the fact that I was good. He always asked a friend to keep an eye on me when I swam to the raft, about a third of a mile out in the Mediterranean. He'd wait patiently, and I can still remember him waving from the beach when I got on the two-story raft. What fun it all was!

"Andrew took such good care of me." Monique had tears in her eyes as she finished telling the story.

Earl put his arms around her. "I'll take good care of you, too," he said.

Twelve

"What am I going to wear for the dinner?" Annie asked aloud, hoping to catch Stanley's attention. He was sitting in his armchair with a lapful of reports, a stack of journals on the floor next to him. Annie repeated the question.

Stanley looked up. "Sure," he answered.

Frustrated, Annie headed toward her closet. It was bursting with colorful, mismatched clothes.

"Stanley, I've got nothing to wear."

Annie was hoping for a consoling comment, but instead she heard another, "Sure, sure," from his corner of their bedroom. Stan was a man of few words, the silent, thinking type. He had a short listening span when he wasn't being a doctor. He'd often say, "Get to the point, Annie." He valued his time. If he weren't reading a journal, he would be improving the aerodynamics of his model electric radio-controlled airplane. Things were different only when they were on vacation, his mind off his professional work and no little airplane to engage his attention.

How simple things had been long ago when she'd first met him. As Annie stared intently into her closet waiting for the right outfit to pop out, she remembered when she had first spotted

Stanley riding the city bus in Berkeley. As she walked down the aisle past him, she noticed how handsome he was. She would have loved to have taken the seat next to him, but she didn't dare. Instead, she sat in the back of the bus so she could study, unobserved, the structure of his head and the frame of his body.

Every time she rode that bus she looked for him, and sometimes she saw him sitting alone, absorbed in a book or just gazing out the window. She began noticing his tanned, muscular physique and his dark brown, neatly combed, wavy hair. Wire-rimmed glasses framed his oval, clean-shaven face. *He's the quiet intellectual type,* she concluded. That quality appealed to Annie.

After riding the bus for a month, always on the lookout for her Prince Charming, she saw him once again. This time he was not alone, but sitting next to her brother's friend Bruce. She found the courage to plop down in front of them and turn around to greet Bruce with a cheerful, "Hi there."

"Annie! Good to see you," Bruce replied. "This is my friend, Stanley." Finally, Stan looked at her. Their eyes met and Annie immediately knew they would be a couple someday.

She should have realized when they were standing at the altar, Stan slumped over, looking very pale and sickly, that she was in for a lifetime challenge. That evening's lightning and thunderstorm after their wedding might have been another omen that life with her new husband was going to be one of constant trials and tribulation. The final warning sign was when the lights in the reception hall shorted out, leaving their guests and bridal party in total darkness. Annie was beginning to realize that her charming knight was perhaps a frog disguised as a handsome prince.

Annie slammed the closet door. "I'm disgusted!" The loud

bang and emotional outburst at last disturbed Stanley. He looked up and made a motion signaling her to calm down. *Men!* Annie thought. *Never a full sentence out of them or a proper reply. After twenty-five years of marriage, you'd think he would have acquired the skill for some decent communication between us.*

This dinner was important to Annie.

Allison and Brad wanted to show her their appreciation for saving Allison. Annie tried to tell Allison that anybody would have gone in and rescued her. It was a natural, automatic response. But Annie did know CPR, and Allison insisted on expressing her gratitude.

Annie was thrilled when Brad had invited them to dinner. She wanted to look her very best and show up as well-groomed as she knew Allison would be. Annie was persistent in her attempts to get Stanley's attention.

"I can't believe we're having dinner with Allison and her husband. It will be so good to see her well again, back to her normal self."

Stanley was still immersed in his papers.

"I'm going to splurge on a new outfit."

Once again, Stanley looked up from his pile of papers and responded with a single syllable. "Sure."

Great, thought Annie. *The third "sure" was the charm. Finally an accurate response. I'm going to find an outfit to match the anniversary purse I bought myself and the shoes I got at the outlet.*

<hr/>

"Honey, do you think Annie and Stan are having trouble finding this restaurant?" Brad asked, looking at his watch again.

"They're twenty minutes late now."

He and Allison sat next to each other at a table for four, with a bottle of champagne on ice. Brad had chosen this casual, but expensive restaurant with a bohemian flair, after Allison told him about avant-garde Annie. It was one of those "nouveau" places near San Pedro Square that prided itself on lighter California cuisine. It was dark inside, with noisy, alcohol-inspired conversation and New Age music. The room was over-decorated, but the tables gleamed with white tablecloths and silver.

The other diners, mostly young, chit-chatted while dallying over their food. The waiters introduced themselves by name, but never seemed to be around when you needed them.

"Knowing Annie," Allison laughed to make light of the situation, "she probably stopped at some store along the way to check for bargains. Or maybe she had a hard time getting Stan to put down his medical journal. From what she tells us, he's an insatiable reader, with his nose always in a book."

"I've got to ask the waiter for appetizers before my stomach starts growling. How about it? He could at least bring us bread and butter," Brad said unhappily.

"Oh, here they come," Allison nudged him as the maitre d' led Annie and her husband to the table. Stan was taller than Allison had expected, graying at the temples, and he wore a conservative navy blue jacket. Annie wore dressy white linen capris with a pink satin inner lining that peeked out at her calves. The scalloped edges of her pants were set off with embroidered flowers in an off-white silk stitch, and her soft pink Irish linen blouse had slits at the sides. Draped around her shoulders was the latest purchase, a long-sleeved black cashmere sweater. The white purse with the multi-colored trim and the shoes she had bought on her way to the women's retreat perfectly completed the outfit.

Annie felt comfortable and confident with her stylish look. "Helloooooo," she cooed, hugging Allison.

Brad rose and shook Stan's outstretched hand. "Welcome," he greeted them.

"How do you do?" Stan said heartily. "And," turning to Allison, "I'm glad to hear you've recovered from your misfortune."

"Thank you, Stan. I hope you didn't have trouble finding this restaurant."

"No, we didn't. The delay was my fault." He helped Annie into a chair and seated himself. "I insisted that we finally buy a new refrigerator, and it took my wife longer than anticipated to choose one. I know that sounds like a lame excuse, but it's the truth."

"Well, you're here now, and that's all that matters," Allison answered. "We've ordered a special meal in Annie's honor tonight. It's a pleasure to finally meet you, Stan. I didn't realize my friend was married to such a distinguished-looking gentleman," she smiled broadly at him.

"Why, thank you, Allison," he accepted her compliment easily. "Annie has spoken about the retreat so much and about all of you ladies who were there. She said the weekend was almost a life-changing event, not that I'd want her to change. She takes such good care of me and the boys.

"And," he went on, "I've been encouraging Annie to get rid of our old fridge for years now, but I think she was particularly attached to it since it was the first appliance we bought after we were married. My wife is very nostalgic."

"Not really," Annie interjected. "I just hate to shop for big appliances."

Allison's eyes widened. "Stan, you mean *you're* the one who wanted a new refrigerator, not Annie?" He nodded. "And all this time I thought she couldn't get you to part with the old one," Allison laughed

"I'd like to make a toast," Brad said, "and then we'll eat — I'm starving!" He filled their glasses and raised his. "To Annie, the wonderful lady who was there to rescue the most important person in my life. Thank you for your alertness, your bravery, and your friendship. I know you mean an awful lot to Allison. Let's drink to Annie!"

"To Annie," Allison declared. They touched glasses and sipped their champagne.

"I wouldn't be here if it hadn't been for your quick thinking. You're my heroine, and I made you this award as a reminder of my appreciation." Allison leaned over and hung a papier-maché gold medal on a blue satin ribbon around Annie's neck and gave her a kiss. The others applauded.

"How clever, Allison! You teachers know all the tricks. This is like winning the Olympics," Annie quipped.

"Here comes the first course, folks. At last!" Brad eyed the waiter as he approached with a large tray. "Allison and I have been here before, so I took the liberty of ordering their excellent cream of turtle soup as a starter."

"Cream of what?" Annie asked. "Did you say what I thought you said, Brad? I could be eating someone's little friend."

"These turtles are farm raised," Brad said.

"Oh, I knew that," Annie said and lifted a spoonful of soup

to her mouth. "Delicious. This is quite a delicacy," she sighed, "and the champagne's superb."

"For the next course," Brad continued, "I've ordered roast duck. I know you'll like it, but don't rush. Enjoy the turtle."

"This is a real pet shop, isn't it?" Annie chuckled.

"Would you rather order something else?" Allison offered. "Please do, Annie. They have wonderful vegetarian dishes, too."

"Thanks, Allison. It's fine. I'm so excited to be here, it doesn't matter what I eat."

"Stan, where did you get your medical training?" Brad asked, dipping a large piece of duck into his orange sauce as soon as he was served.

"I joined the Army after the Korean War. It was the only way I could afford medical school. But as it turned out, I enjoyed the service. We were between wars, thankfully."

"I was at Lackland Air Force Base, in Texas, about that time," Brad explained. "I was assigned to write a manual on radar."

The men began comparing notes on life in the military. While their husbands traded stories, Annie told Allison about her Chinese watercolor class. "I'm learning the ancient brush techniques," she beamed. "I love it. Fish, flowers and bamboo."

After they'd finished their main course and the table had been cleared, Allison clapped her hands. "Everybody, a special dessert is on its way with our coffee. Chocolate mousse!"

"Chocolate sounds divine, as long as it's 'mousse' and not 'mouse,'" Annie smiled. "What a treat! It pays to be a hero."

The photo looked familiar and the name "Allison Boyce" seemed to jump out of the newspaper at Carol. "I can't believe it," she murmured to herself. *That's Allison — our Allison and the Jonas story she read at the luncheon. In the magazine section of the Sunday newspaper!*
Carol was leisurely reading the Mercury over her second cup of morning coffee. She remembered there had been some talk after the luncheon about the possibility of publication of the story Allison had told them, and maybe even publication of the other stories of human courage and caring that Allison had been collecting for some time.

"The Sunday magazine section!" Carol exclaimed aloud. *Not a throwaway. For this you get paid. That's arrival, I'd say. I wonder if Allison knows her story has been published.*

Carol reached for her address book. Allison's line was busy, so she called Josephine. Josephine would love to know. *I hope she's home, so I don't have to leave a message.* The phone rang two, then three times. On the fourth ring, Jo picked up.

"Hi, Josephine. This is Carol. Have you seen today's paper?"

"No, not yet. Why? What's up?"

"Well, go get the magazine section. Allison's story is in there."

"Hold it a sec. The paper's here, on top of my work table," Jo said. Carol could hear her shuffling papers. "Oh you're right! Allison didn't know exactly when they were going to publish it."

"How's she doing, by the way?"

"Looking beautiful, and she and Brad are trying hard to sort things out."

"I called her before you, just now, but I couldn't get through.

And I had to share the news with someone. I still want to call her and see if she knows that she's famous. In print. Unless you want to be the bearer of the good news?"

"No, you call. She'll be happy to hear from you, Carol," Josephine assured her. "But since I have you on the line, I need a dinner recipe — a really special one. I'm having a dinner guest. I was looking in my cookbooks, but I didn't find the right entree. I think I'd like to do a pasta dish."

"Pasta? Oh, yes, I have a wonderful recipe for linguine with a fantastic sauce — cream, dill and pine nuts. I'll get it to you pronto. And don't forget a bottle of dry red wine, although if he's a gentleman, he should bring the bottle. My favorite is Cabernet Sauvignon."

"Wines I know, Carol. I just need help with the food. And what makes you think it's a "he" I'm having over?"

Carol cleared her throat and laughed. "He wouldn't be someone we all met this past spring, would he?"

Jo laughed too. "And I thought we were being so discreet," she feigned despondency.

Allison picked up the phone on the first ring. Was she home alone? Carol wondered.

"Allison, this is Carol."

"Hi, honey. So sweet of you to call. How are you?"

"Do you know you're in today's magazine section of the newspaper? You and Jonas. Your story has been published."

"What? Where?"

"You haven't heard, haven't seen it?"

"No. They said I would get paid when the story was published, but they didn't say when that would be. I was beginning to worry they might never publish it, just sit on it. Having it in print is more important than the money. Although, of course, that's good, too."

"It's in today's Mercury News. You're a professional writer now, Allison," Carol paused. "This calls for a celebration!"

"Oh, don't be silly, Carol!"

"It does. And anyway, I've been looking for an occasion to get all of us together again, and now I've found one. We bonded well, and that is not something to treat lightly. It isn't often that women — and some of us were total strangers before — can click like that, be supportive and grow so fond of one another."

"Well, okay, since you put it like that. My female friendships have become more precious to me since I've gotten older. There's truth to that, Carol."

"I've discovered that it's friends you can count on to rejoice with when things are going well, and friends, more than family, who help you over the rough spots. So, Allison, I'm going to call the others and arrange something at my house, maybe next week. Do you have a preference as to which day?"

"No. I'm sticking close to home lately, so any day you choose is fine with me. Call Jo and see what her TV schedule is like. Let me know, Carol. And thanks. Especially for that wisdom about female friends."

When the details had been arranged, Carol called Maevis and told her about Allison's story being published and the celebration. Bring Neal, too, she told Maevis.

"I'm sho ex-shy-ted fuh huh." Maevis was trying to speak. She held Chloe's hair clip between her teeth as she arranged the child's pony tails. "Allishon deshrves zish. The Jonash shtory wush well-written and very tushing."

"Uh, pardon me?"

"Sorry," Maevis removed the metal fastener from her mouth. "I said, Allison deserves this. Her Jonas story was very touching. Besides, we women need to have our own successes, independent of the men. And when we do, why not celebrate?"

"Maevis, I love your old-time feminist banter. You're so secure in who you are," Carol praised.

"Not as much as you might think, Carol. I put on a good act. I love parties, but I don't really think Allison will be happy to see me."

"Maevis, of course she will. Put those negative thoughts out of your head," Carol replied.

"Okay, if you say so. And I can tell Annie. I'm going to see her at the rink tomorrow. Hey, why don't you come to the rink too, Carol? You're doing so well. All your old skating moves are coming right back. I hope Annie doesn't forget. She is busy with something called Chinese brush painting these days. Come on, Carol, meet us there."

"I might take you up on that, as long as you don't mind having an old lady around."

"Carol, you're the coolest older woman I know, and you're a blast to be with."

"Thanks. I've one more piece of info, but keep it under your hat, Maevis. It's nothing official yet, and it's not my news to spread."

"What? Tell me quick, I love gossip — oops! — I mean news."

"I think something's cooking between Josephine and Jack."

"Josephine and who?"

"Jack. From the spa. Remember Mr. Masseur? Tall, dark and... the owner's son?"

"How could I forget him? Tall, dark and I wanted him for myself — if I weren't married, of course."

"No pun intended about something cooking, but Josephine asked me for a recipe. Said someone special was coming for dinner."

"Carol, do you think they got it on at the spa?"

"Maevis! You have a one-track mind!" Carol laughed.

"What's "goddidon," Mommy?" Carol heard little Chloe's voice.

Maevis shrieked. "I have to go, Carol! See you at the rink."

Thirteen

"Allison, hi. It's Jo."

"Jo, honey," said Allison in her unique way. The voice of recognition was warm, and Josephine felt covered by its intimacy. "You rarely have time to call me between our Saturday brunches. Is everything okay?"

"Things are fine. Well, not really." After hearing Allison's voice, Josephine almost forgot why she had called. "I'm calling to tell you something very important and not so pleasant. You know all the trouble I've been having walking, the stumbling. Well, I've finally got a diagnosis, and it isn't good. I have MS — multiple sclerosis. I wanted you to know. And I had to get it out — quickly."

Josephine was quiet for a few long moments, to let her friend take in what she had said. Actually, Jo was listening to herself say the words. She hadn't said them to anybody else yet, and the experience was new for her. She assumed that her friend knew as much about MS as she did — zilch.

"That's why I don't walk well and my hands are numb... and I have to run to the bathroom a lot."

"Are you sure of the diagnosis?" Allison asked.

"Yes. It was verified by an MRI."

"What's going to happen? Will it get worse?" At least Allison didn't tell her to take up meditation or get off wheat.

"I'm not sure. There are two kinds, they tell me. One, people go in and out of remission. With the other, things get worse."

Allison asked tentatively, "What kind do you have?"

"I don't know yet. I hope the first kind."

"What can they do for you?"

"There is no medication yet. They're working on it, doing a lot of research."

"Oh, Jo. I'm so sorry to hear this. How did you find out?" asked Allison.

"Well, I finally went to another doctor, and he sent me for the tests. As I said, it was confirmed by an MRI. I do have it." Josephine was so relieved to finally have a diagnosis that her voice had a tinge of happiness and a serious tone at the same time. These were feelings at cross purposes — elated to end the mystery, but devastated to find out there was no cure.

Josephine had to tell Allison about the MS because... because... why? Could it be true that Jo really believed that Allison's love and friendship would shield her?

"The symptoms began last year after Papa died. The first doctor I saw recommended a shrink."

"I remember when you told me. I knew *that* was wrong. Honey, do you want me to come over?"

Josephine declined, saying she needed to call the rest of her friends. Papa's dying and the symptoms becoming full-blown had something to do with telephoning her friends. Papa's protective love was gone, and all this wouldn't have happened if he had still been here. That at least is what Jo thought. And she knew her friends. They wouldn't gasp at the news, thereby scaring her further. They would listen; she could count on them.

Josephine drove into the parking lot at KTRS. "To tell or not to tell... that is the question." She grinned at her thought, but it was not a mirthful grin. Sam, with his reporter's nose, had probably already guessed something was up, just watching her walk. She had the urge to park in one of the handicapped spots. It was closer to the front doors. She didn't dare. Besides getting a huge ticket, people knew her car, and there would be questions she wasn't prepared to answer.

Letting her boss know about the MS was something she definitely wasn't looking forward to. She loved her job, but going out to report the news was increasingly becoming too difficult. Would Sam just say, "Sorry, but good-bye"? What would she do if she lost this job? Jo just couldn't bear the thought of that.

Sam greeted her as she entered the newsroom and he at once began lauding her latest report. *Tell him now...TELL HIM NOW.* The directive came louder and louder.

"Do you have a minute, Sam? I have something to tell you that is pretty serious."

"Sure, Josephine." Sam led her to an alcove, and they sat down. No one was around. "What's up?"

"I've been to a neurologist and had an MRI, two reliable sources according to any good reporter. And I hate to say it, but it seems I have multiple sclerosis."

"Whew!" Sam wiped his forehead with his handkerchief. "So that's what's been causing the changes I've noticed in you lately. I didn't want to say anything until you brought it up,

Josephine. I'm so sorry."

"I'm having a hard time walking steadily, and you know that going out into the field requires a lot of walking." Josephine swallowed hard. *There. I've done it. I've told Sam, and the ceiling is still up there. It hasn't fallen down on my head yet.* She looked at her boss, whom she had always admired and trusted. Sam was deep in thought and his brows were furrowed. His concern for her was obvious.

"Speaking formally as the manager, we'll have to think about how that impacts your work here. But Josephine, you have so much talent; I will not have it lost to this station. We'll come up with a plan to keep you with us, doing whatever you can do. I can see that your mind and your smile aren't affected."

"So far at least, no, but I've been told that I could end up in a wheelchair."

"Well, then, you can certainly anchor from a wheelchair. Our audience knows you and loves you. Let me ponder this for a while and see what we can figure out. For now, let's have you and Diane change places. She's been on my back to go out in the field, and you can take over her work here."

"Thank you, Sam, so much. I'll get with Diane as soon as she comes in, and we can coach each other so it will be a smooth transition."

As Sam hurried out, Josephine sighed deeply. Her hands were shaking, and it wasn't from MS. She sat for a minute longer and waited for her heartbeat to return to normal.

<hr>

It was a bright, sunny day and Monique felt she just had to

be out doing something, so she called Carol. "Would you like to meet me at Montalvo? It's too gorgeous to spend the day indoors." Monique loved the beautiful estate: the Mediterranean mansion, its lush gardens, and especially the hiking trails.

"I'd love to. I was just about to walk around in the neighborhood, but Montalvo would be much prettier," Carol said.

"In forty-five minutes?"

"Sure thing. I'm already dressed for it."

They met at the number two parking lot. "My gosh, you've lost weight!" Monique exclaimed when Carol got out of her car. "You look magnificent, and I love the color of your hair. Has your daughter seen the new you?" Immediately she regretted bringing up Felice. Why upset Carol on such a lovely day?

"We had dinner a few nights ago. She approved of the weight loss, but I was expecting her to suggest a different hair color," Carol laughed softly. "She usually finds something negative to say, and she's a nut about hair."

Changing the subject, Monique asked, "How are your plans coming along for Allison's celebration? What can I do to help you?" They walked toward the trail head behind the mansion.

"Everything's under control, but I'll let you know if we need anything. My friend Dottie is helping me. She's the grandmother of the girl I wrote about at the journaling workshop. I'm so pleased you and Earl can make it. Everyone's coming, and it'll be so nice to get together again." Carol paused. "Josephine has spoken to you, hasn't she?"

"Yes. She's called all of us. MS — it's terrible, isn't it? I'm glad she found out what the problem is, but now all we can do is stand by and support her."

"Yes, it is awful. I think she's got something good in her life, though, to counter that terrible news. It's just a hunch, Monique, but I think she has a boyfriend."

"Really?"

"She asked me for a recipe. I gave her one of my favorites with pasta and pine nuts. She said she was entertaining a special someone. I think it's that fellow from the spa. The tall one with the dark hair. Remember him?"

"Oh, yes. He was certainly good looking and seemed considerate. But personally, I wouldn't want Ursula for my mother-in-law."

"Monique, I've never heard you make a disparaging remark about anyone!"

"I don't usually, but there are some people who rub me the wrong way."

"I suppose if we had to be enamored of the betrothed's entire family, not many of us would ever marry," Carol replied pensively.

"Probably not," Monique agreed. "You know, on one of my hikes I heard an old Italian proverb about pine nuts. Apparently it is said that if you cook a man a dish with pine nuts, he'll love you forever."

Carol laughed. "I'll pass that information on to Josephine. She'll be glad to hear it."

"Yes, she will," Monique said. "And I don't know whether it's true or not, but just in case it is, Carol, would you please send me a copy of the recipe, too?"

Carol laughed again. "You don't need to cook with pine nuts, Monique, to get anyone to love you forever."

They walked at a brisk pace. The trail was dusty. Other hikers were coming down the steep hill that they were beginning to climb, so the two friends went single file. Now, in spite of slowing down, Carol was out of breath. At the top of the ridge, they stopped to take in the gorgeous view of the southern section of the San Francisco Bay. "Look there," Monique pointed off in the distance to two massive airplane hangars that were big enough to accommodate a blimp, "that's Moffett Field."

"Let's sit a few minutes," Carol moved to a convenient tree stump. "This change in altitude is hard on me."

"It's nice up here," Monique said, still standing, "and so peaceful."

"Umm," Carol agreed. They were silent and took in the view until Carol spoke again. "Did you work after your husband died, Monique?" she asked.

"Oh, yes, I had to. I was already a French teacher at a private school near here, and I continued teaching there for several more years."

"The thing that is most gratifying to me about working at the shelter," Carol said, "isn't helping the women as much as it is making the children feel more secure."

"Yes, and I found it wonderful to see the light go on in a child's mind when he or she finally understands something you have been trying to explain," Monique concurred. "People are surprised sometimes, but middle school was my favorite age group."

"I can't believe that twelve and thirteen year olds would top anyone's list."

"It's true. They are. At lunch time, I would sit in my

classroom and converse in French with some of the eighth graders. There was one boy I especially liked. The day after graduation the whole eighth grade always went to Great America, and this particular boy asked his parents to invite me along on the class trip. What an honor, I felt, to be chosen as a favorite teacher by a thirteen year old boy.

"'Madame, you have to come with us on the Turn of the Century,' he told me when we got to the park. Do you know Great America, Carol?"

"Believe it or not, Monique, I've never been there. Amusement parks didn't appeal to Felice."

"Having met your daughter, I can believe that," Monique smiled at Carol. "The Turn of the Century is a wild roller coaster. There I was, this middle-aged widow, surrounded by youngsters, getting into the car of a roller coaster known to be terribly frightening. Well, after the first ride, during which I screamed as much as they did, the young people asked me to go on again and again. I went on the ride with them seven times, and I felt like a thirteen-year-old myself. I wondered what was wrong with me!"

"Didn't any of the other adults go on the rides besides you?"

"No. I was the only adult on that thrill seeker's roller coaster. The mothers all waited nearby at a small cafe, sipping iced lemonade. When we returned, laughing loudly, they looked at me with a mixture of surprise and envy. 'How could you stand it, Madame?' one asked me."

"I couldn't have stood it either," Carol said.

"I was so happy during the rides that I forgot for a moment that I was supposed to be a dignified teacher. As the afternoon progressed, I returned to normal and became again the person I felt deep inside myself, a person who was lonely and carried a heavy sadness."

"Oh, Monique," Carol commiserated. "But I can picture you jumping around with the teenagers. You're not that much taller than most of them, and I can believe that they would love you and feel at ease with you."

"Thank you. I loved them, too — and teaching," Monique sighed.

"What do you say we start down?" Carol stood and stretched.

"But instead of going back the way we came," Monique suggested, "why don't we continue along the top of the Redwood Trail and come down by the creek? It's a route I've taken with the Sierra Club, and I think you'll like it."

"It'll certainly be easier for me than the Turn of the Century," Carol laughed.

—◈◦◈—

Ursula was sitting across from Josephine. They were having lunch at Roma Bella in downtown San Jose. Ursula was dressed all in black, down to the black stockings that went into her black patent leather pumps. Her black blouse was silky and elegant. Her hair was pulled back in a chignon. Josephine had a foreboding. She was lunching with a vampire bat. She and Ursula eyed each other. They ordered their meal: salads and a glass of white wine for each. Jo nibbled at the popovers that had been placed at her elbow, but Ursula wasted no time.

"Do you think it's fair to marry my son knowing that you have a disease that may leave you incapacitated in the future and totally dependent on others — especially Jack — for your care?

Oh yes! You're a beautiful and vivacious woman now, but what do you think lies down the road? Have you thought about that? I have. I think that you are being selfish — with *my son*."

Ursula took a sip of her wine, put the glass down and fixed Josephine with an unwavering stare. There it was. The worst of Jo's fears spoken aloud. And now this woman could stand in the way of her being with Jack.

"I love Jack," Josephine said simply. "None of us knows for sure what life has to offer, and whatever it is, we want to meet it together."

"I don't want that kind of pain for my son. I don't want him to have to lead you around, clean commodes or have to visit his wife in a nursing home one day."

The sleeves of Ursula's black silk blouse spread into the wings of a giant creature and she began to rise. She flew circles around the chandelier, a shrill "eeeeeeeeee" coming from her lips.

Jo felt her body get very heavy. A knot of fear tied up her stomach as she watched Ursula navigate the room and land back in her seat. Josephine tried to fly, but her body was too heavy. It would not go up. She tried and tried. Her malady was oppressive. It would not permit her the necessary lightness of being. She could not take off. Ursula rose into the air again.

Josephine wanted to die. *I want the MS out of my life right now!* She felt so hopeless. Ursula was flying above her. Ursula was right, SHE WAS RIGHT! Josephine had no business trying to tie her beloved Jack to this kind of hopelessness and despair.

Jo still could not take off from her seat. Inside somewhere she began to cry. "But I wanted to marry Jack and have children," she sobbed.

Ursula stopped in mid-flight. "Children?" she repeated. "Did you say children?" Ursula's silky blouse began changing from black to irridescent blue. Color appeared in her cheeks. She descended into the chair. Josephine thought she saw a turning up at the corners of Ursula's lips. Her wings were gone now and a rainbow appeared.

"Here is your salad, Ma'am," a voice said from somewhere, and then Josephine heard, "The temperature in San Jose is 61 degrees, partly cloudy..."

Jo opened her eyes. The clock radio glowed 6:45. It was a new day.

———◆◆———

Monique had just come back from her late morning walk and was standing at the kitchen counter slicing a hardboiled egg for her famous Shrimp Louie salad. These efforts to fix a good lunch reminded her of the time last year when she'd invited Earl for dinner. She had made salmon, but Earl did not want to eat it. "Why not?" she had asked, a bit miffed.

"Because it's not cooked enough. I need my salmon almost dry," he answered without hesitation. "Next time I will cook a meal for you, and if you really want salmon, just wait till I prepare my best recipe. I'm an excellent cook, you know." Earl had been true to his word. The salmon he made for her at his apartment a week later was perfect. Monique knew she was dealing with a real pro, and was putting together the Shrimp Louie now just the way he liked it.

Earl was going to retire soon from his work in Burlingame and said he could then come and see her more often. She knew he was lonely in his apartment since his brother died a few years ago. Earl was so kind and warm towards her that she could not help feeling contented and secure around him, and Monique had made up her mind to ask him today to live with her in her small house for the rest of their lives.

Earl had been a bachelor all his life. He had spent four years in the army during World War II and had fought the Germans in Monte Casino in Italy. Upon returning from overseas, he developed painful gout because of the food he ate during the long years in the service. As a result of his health problems, he never married. He had trouble standing for long periods of time, until finally, a doctor found the right medication to lessen the joint swellings in his feet. Earl became a chiropractor, but still his gout would flare up and prevent him from working regularly. Fortunately he had been frugal and had saved enough money to buy a small apartment building. Now he had a comfortable income from the rental of his flats.

When Earl arrived at Monique's, he greeted her with a bouquet of flowers and a big hug. She knew that she was making the right decision, and blurted it out immediately.

"Sweetheart, do you want to come live with me here in my house?"

"Monique," he laughed, "I'm taken aback. What's gotten into you all of a sudden?"

"Well, I thought that pretty soon when you retire, you won't have to get up early in the morning to go to your practice, so you could live here in Los Gatos with me."

"I'd love to live with you, but there are some things that would have to be taken care of first."

"What do you mean? You're free to do as you please, aren't you?"

"Of course I am, but I have a big responsibility with the apartment building and my tenants who count on me to keep up the place."

Monique hadn't expected this response, but quickly came up with a solution. "Well, you could get a property manager and put him or her in charge. The manager will collect the rents for you each month in exchange for a lower rent. And you can go visit your sister as often as you like while I am busy with my usual activities."

"I will have to pay more in taxes the day I want to sell my building, if I don't live there anymore, you know."

"I guess I didn't think of that," said Monique grimly, afraid that Earl would never agree to come and live with her. After they had finished coffee and dessert, he pulled Monique onto his lap.

"Remember I said before that if I don't live in my apartment building, I will have to pay a lot more taxes when I sell it?" She nodded. "That's true. But my heart is saying, 'Don't be such a miser.' " He kissed her on the cheek. "Let me think about it for a while."

Later, as they were finishing the dishes, Earl came close to Monique, nuzzled her on the neck and said, "Mon chou, I have thought it over. My feelings for you are so strong that I cannot think of living away from you. You'll see that we'll always be able to manage the financial difficulties somehow. Other seniors do. Let's live the rest of our lives together and to heck with the money."

Fourteen

Josephine and Jack sat holding hands on a park bench by the ocean in Pacific Grove. Jack had asked her to come down from San Jose and meet him there. He wanted to discuss her refusal of his marriage proposal. They loved each other, that much they both knew. Ever since their getaway to Big Sur, this love had been the one sure thing between them. Now, weeks later, when Jack was wanting her to set a date to join their lives together, Josephine had said no and she'd given him back the ring.

"Why, Jo? Why?"

"There's no way. My future is too uncertain. I can't burden you with this disease," she said plaintively. "Oh, I hate this. Hate it!"

A friendly chipmunk came by at their feet. "Do we have some crumbs to share with him?" Josephine was grateful for the momentary distraction.

"Jo, please don't be this way," Jack said tenderly.

Tears sprang to Josephine's eyes, and she buried her head in his chest.

"Jo, we could have such a beautiful life together."

"With you pushing me around in a wheelchair? I don't know what I'll be like ten years down the road."

"Ten years down the road, Jo, we'll love each other even more. We're not a fly-by-night operation here. I'm in it for the long haul. We'll handle whatever comes along together." Jack turned Jo to face him and lifted her chin. "Together, darling."

She couldn't stop the tears. Jack tried to slip the ring back on her finger. Her hand was trembling.

"Don't make your final decision yet," Jack pleaded. "I have an idea. You must meet my friends Seymour and Beverly."

"And why must I?"

"You'll see why. Just promise you'll come with me to meet them." The chipmunk jumped onto the bench next to them. "Look at this audacious little guy!" Jack said.

Jo rummaged through her purse. "I might have something for him." She rolled a piece of a peanut butter sandwich into a ball and held it out on the palm of her hand. The chipmunk got up on its hind legs and snatched the tidbit.

Josephine had her tears under control now and turned back to face Jack. The ocean waves crashed against the rocks. Foam and water shot high into the air in a festive display. "It's so lovely here," Jo murmured with her head on her beloved's shoulder.

"Yes, it is," he said softly into her golden hair. The chipmunk scampered away. "It's because I love you so much, Jo, that I can't let you face this alone. You're not the only person who's ever had a chronic disease and a relationship at the same time. I need you, too — as you are, and as you will be. I understand what could happen. I love you, Jo. I love your soul. We can handle this together."

True to his word, Jack had telephoned his friends Beverly and Seymour, and they had immediately issued a warm invitation for him and Josephine to come over.

"This is a beautiful house, Beverly, and dinner was scrumptious." Josephine was helping clear the table after the meal, while Beverly rinsed dishes at a sink that had been lowered to accommodate her wheelchair. Everything in the kitchen was custom-designed, the cupboards lowered so she could reach in and pull things out. Jo was overwhelmed and frightened by it all. Would she, too, need a kitchen like this one day?

"I had polio as a young girl," Beverly said simply and matter-of-factly, as if she were telling Josephine that she'd had measles. "I was in an iron lung for almost a year." She sighed. "It was a long time ago."

"When did you and Seymour get married? How old were you?"

"I was twenty-five."

"But, how did you...?" Jo stopped. There was so much she wanted to know, but it seemed rude to blurt out her questions.

"How did we decide to get married? How did we manage?" guessed Beverly. "It wasn't easy." She swung her chair toward the open patio door. "Let's go outside where it's cool."

Beverly wheeled herself down the wide wooden ramp out to a shady spot and Jo followed, pulling over a garden chair to be near the other woman. Jack and Seymour were still inside in the living room engrossed in their own conversation. Jo could hear their voices and, she imagined, the tinkling of ice inside their glasses.

"What do you think of me and Jack getting married,

considering that I have MS and it may get much worse with time?"

"That's entirely your decision. I can't make that choice for you."

"I've been telling Jack, 'No,' but he said I should come here and meet you before I make my final decision."

"Josephine," Beverly resumed after a few moments of silence, "we've known Jack since he attended high school with our son, Charles. He'd stop by here almost everyday, just like it was his own home. We're family."

"How many children do you and Seymour have?"

"Four."

"Wow."

"Josephine, getting married is the easy part. Even having the kids was relatively simple, compared with raising them. The most difficult part was staying married, and that's the hard part whether one has a chronic illness or not. What really matters are your feelings for Jack and what he feels for you. I'm not saying that love conquers all, but it's certainly a top priority. Respect comes next. From the little I've seen of you two together, I think you have the ingredients. Now you have to decide if you want to make the pie." Beverly smiled at Josephine. "You *do* have a right to the pie, dear, remember that. You're a person, too. You may be an ill person, but multiple sclerosis does not mean your life is over. My life would have been so much the poorer if I had given up fifty years ago when I got polio."

———

Allison listened carefully. *Was that the doorbell?* She wasn't expecting anyone. Perhaps it was one of those door-to-door solicitors. She half-opened the front door and was surprised to see Maevis standing on the step looking ill at ease, clutching a potted plant.

"Maevis, what are you doing here?" Allison blurted out. "I mean, this is such a surprise. We haven't seen each other since..." She stopped abruptly and then, gathering herself, said warmly, "Come in, please come in."

"Are you sure? This isn't a bad time or anything?"

"No, not at all. You're looking great, Maevis!" Allison hurriedly picked up some scattered newspapers and fluffed a pillow on the sofa. "Is this a get-well visit? I'm really doing much better now."

"Here, I've brought you a plant." Maevis thrust it into Allison's hands.

"Why, it's beautiful! Thank you. What pretty ruffled leaves!"

"The Latin name is *ocimum basilicum,* better known as 'basil.' This kind's a bit fancier. It's a companion plant for toma-toes. It's supposed to help them grow better. You have tomatoes don't you?"

"Of course. But a companion plant? How interesting."

"Yes, some plants thrive when their friends are nearby."

"Like people." Allison's eyes met Maevis' for a second. "I'll get a coaster and keep it right here on the coffee table for the time being. Later, I'll plant it outside and see whether my tomatoes look happier," Allison said, going into another room.

It took all of Maevis' determination not to bolt while Allison was away. Maevis was extremely uncomfortable about this visit, but she'd forced herself to come. Despite Allison's friendly attitude, Maevis wasn't certain that Allison would be receptive to her agenda. Maevis intended to bring up her own behavior at the pool that Saturday morning at the retreat and to beg Allison's forgiveness.

"It's a lovely plant, thanks again," Allison reiterated when she came back with a cork trivet which she placed under the pot. "But it's unnecessary. I've been almost one hundred percent well for awhile now." She glanced at her one-time antagonist curiously, but stopped short of asking Maevis directly why she had come.

"I heard from the others that you were doing better, and I'm really glad." Maevis sat on the edge of the sofa. "This isn't exactly a get-well visit, though. I have some other things on my mind, but it's so hard to get started. Could you just listen until I get it all out before you say anything? Or else I'm afraid I won't be able to make myself sound sane."

"Of course. I'll close these doors so we won't be disturbed. My husband's working in the back."

Maevis began with her childhood in Philadelphia, her Catholic school upbringing, then her escape to Berkeley. By the time she got to the years with Alex, she had picked up steam like a runaway locomotive. She was ready to blurt out the details of their recent miserable reunion after he'd visited Allison in the hospital, and how he made her take the bus back from wherever they were, and what an awful, self-absorbed deadbeat he was, and how she was no longer hung up on him, and how he hadn't ever been good enough for someone like Allison… but fortunately Maevis restrained herself. She emphasized, instead, her current roles of mother and faithful wife, dominant themes of her past twelve years. She revealed the bad feelings that plagued her as a result of the Monterey weekend. She apologized for causing

Allison grief. She cried.

Allison listened to Maevis' narrative without interruption. When Maevis finally wound down and ran out of words, Allison said softly, "I'm glad you had the courage to come over. There have been a lot of misunderstandings between us. Let me give you a hug for being brave enough to tell me all this. I'm not certain I would have been able to do what you have done.

"Truthfully, Maevis, some of the hurts still remain with me. But you have cleared up a lot of things. And as long as you have been so up-front, I have a few things to tell you myself."

Maevis nodded, sniffling into her tissue.

"I have been in therapy since... since before the spa. God knows I needed it. My therapist is wonderful, and she helped me realize a very important truth. I have been mourning, yes mourning, the loss of Alex. As you have come to realize yourself, he isn't really worth anyone's tears." She smiled a little bitterly.

"But all these years, I have more seriously been mourning the death of that marriage. Oh, I know, it's silly in these days of one divorce for every three weddings, but at that time I didn't know any person who had ever been divorced. To tell the truth, appearances and my reputation have always been way too important to me. It's something I'm trying to put in perspective. And I always felt that everyone was talking about the fact that I had been left, that I hadn't been a good wife."

"You can't run your life on what others think," Maevis spoke up. "I found that out, too."

"Intellectually, I know that, but emotionally I still want to have a blemish-free reputation. Then there were other things going on as well. I acted as though I hated your free and easy ways, but I may have been envious of how you make your life work. Alex and I married young, had three children in quick succession, and then I had to raise them alone. There was suddenly no one else to be the adult but me. I tried to make the kids' lives as normal as if their Dad hadn't left. I couldn't afford to do anything even slightly wild. I had to look and act respectable all the time, so no one would talk about me. And even worse, I set excessively high standards for the kids, too, for just the same reason."

"I know," Maevis said with empathy, "we generally expect more of our own family than we do of others."

"I'm beginning to realize that now. At the time, I wanted to march at some of the war protests, but I felt I couldn't afford to, although in my heart I am very liberal. I would have liked to have worn flowing, flowery clothes and sandals, but I was divorced and I couldn't stand any more taint. When I first met you, I immediately pegged you for all the things that had been denied me, and I was just too jealous to let you be my friend."

"A lot of this long hair and turquoise is just for show," Maevis laughed. "I'm not nearly as much of a hippie as you might think."

"I know that now, but my grudge against you was instant. After we talked at the pool and you told me you had been Alex's girlfriend, I saw you making the others laugh at dinner, and I was certain you were telling them intimate things about me that you had heard from him."

"Allison, I was as shocked as you were to learn we had both been with Alex. And I would never have said anything to the others. No, we were laughing about something else, but you jumped to conclusions. I can understand why."

Allison continued. "Then I was going through this thing with Brad. I guess I just had a lot of misconceptions. I may look as if I'm this all-together lady, but I just wear that mask to cover up what's really inside. The therapy has helped me see this."

Maevis jumped up and gave Allison a hug. "I'm not nearly as unconventional as I look, and now it seems that you're not as straight as you look. Hey, I'm so glad I came over, and I'm thankful that you listened and let me explain. I was feeling so guilty."

"I don't know about men, but I think we women are especially vulnerable in our early years, and we tend to crumble too easily. Then, some survival instinct pushes us to put all the pieces together again. Most of the time we emerge stronger. I've known some pretty tough cookies. I think the two of us qualify." Allison laughed. "Speaking of, how about some cookies and soda, or milk, or a beer? Want to share one? We can skip the cookies..."

Fifteen

"Josephine and Jack, come and meet my hubby!" Maevis stood with a bottle of wine in her hand in the foyer of Carol's old Victorian home. "Neal and I are just going to the kitchen to uncork the wine."

"It's 'cork' the wine, baby," Neal quietly corrected her.

"You're kidding!" Maevis raised one eyebrow. "That sounds weird to me. Look, Nealsy, you say it your way, and I'll say it mine," she grinned. "Josephine, do you and Jack want to come with us into the kitchen? The more the merrier!" Maevis was gone before they could reply, trailing a hint of patchouli oil behind her.

"Your wife's a character, Neal," Josephine said pleasantly, "and we wouldn't have her any other way. But *you* keep her company in the kitchen. Jack and I want to go outside and see Carol's beautiful garden."

Neal followed Maevis into the kitchen where she picked up an old-fashioned corkscrew. They had been the first ones to arrive at Carol's party. Their babysitter lived just down the street in the same Rose Garden neighborhood off the Alameda. They'd left Chloe and the twins only fifteen minutes before. When Carol opened her door to them, Maevis introduced Neal, giving her husband the lowdown on how well she and Carol had clicked from the moment they'd met at the BACC luncheon. "Carol feels like a long-lost sister, we get along so well," Maevis told him.

"Or rather," Carol revised the assessment, "you feel more like a second daughter to me, one who doesn't try to manage my life," she laughed.

Now, a new voice at the door called out cheerfully, "Hello, Carol!" Monique kissed the hostess on both cheeks, hugged her earnestly, and presented a gentleman in a green tie with a leprechaun's twinkle in his eye.

"This must be Earl," Carol said and shook his hand. "Actually, I remember when you and Monique met," she told him. "I was there with her that night at the dance."

"I'm sorry, I don't remember you. I only had eyes for Monique." Earl grinned.

Maevis came out of the kitchen carrying a tray of wine glasses and an open bottle of red wine. "It's breeeathing," she announced, nodding to the bottle and affecting a snooty connoisseur's voice. "And whom might this charming gentleman be?" she asked coquettishly.

"Maevis," Monique beamed, "this is my dear friend, Earl Leonard."

"*Enchantée*," Maevis curtsied carefully. A glass wobbled on the tray.

"Let's go into the living room," Carol suggested. "We've prepared some hors d'oeuvres for you to have with the wine."

"I can't believe how lovely your home is, Carol," Maevis said more seriously. "The long flagstone walkway makes me feel as if I'm entering an old European palace. And look at these wonderful hardwood floors and the bay window," she gushed. "Don't tell me you have an attic too and dormer windows that capture the afternoon sun?" She batted her lashes coyly. "I confess that's not original. I read it in a book somewhere."

"As a matter of fact, Maevis," Carol laughed, "the window seat in the upstairs hall is my favorite place to curl up with a good mystery. This house is a hundred years old. It was built in 1886, and it has many nooks and crannies. I haven't said much about my home because I wasn't sure if I'd sell it and move to a smaller place or not.

"But things have changed recently. Remember Margaret, the teenager in the story I wrote at the spa? Well, she and her grandmother, Dottie, are now my housemates. They're living here with me, and they've been a great help in the preparations for this party, though they've gone out for the night.

I'll give you the complete house tour when the others show up, if you like," she offered.

"Oh, there's the bell again." Carol went into the foyer. "Help yourselves to the appetizers and get Neal to pour more Cabernet," she called back to them.

"What an elaborate buffet she has prepared for us!" said Monique. "And look at that old upright piano over there, Earl. I'm sure you'd love to get your fingers on it, wouldn't you?"

"It is a work of art," Earl said, running his hands along the wood. Then he struck a few keys. "And it's in tune — amazing for an instrument this old."

"These dolmas are amazing, too," Maevis mumbled with a full mouth. "I wonder what Carol's put in them. Definitely non-traditional."

"Earl would be able to tell you," Monique boasted. "He's a wonderful cook." She bit into a finger-sized stuffed grape leaf and put the rest up to Earl's lips. He chewed without removing his fingers from the piano and smacked his lips appreciatively.

"I think it's crab with tarragon," he said, "and I taste garlic, too."

"*Quel gourmet!*" Monique approved.

"Our guests of honor everyone — the famous author and her husband," Carol called out, ushering Allison & Brad into the living room.

Carol glanced around. Who was missing? Josephine and Jack must still be in the garden, but what about Annie and her husband? Annie was always late. Carol had also invited Felice. Would her daughter show up? For an exacting attorney, Felice could be very unreliable socially.

The bell chimed again. Carol opened the door expecting to see an apologetic, excuse-laden Annie, but instead it was Felice. Sylvie stood at her side, smiling, and she held out her hand. "Hi, Carol. I hope I'm not intruding."

"No, of course not. You're always welcome in my home, Sylvie."

"I'm eager to hear about the changes you are going to make, now that you've decided to keep the house," Sylvie said. "Felice told me."

"It's mostly the kitchen," Carol answered. "I'll show you the detailed plans another time when you come over. It'll be a month before they can get started anyway. I'm going to keep the original flavor of the period, but update the appliances, cabinets and floor."

Carol liked Felice's friend Sylvie. She was down-to-earth, realistic, and she exuded warmth. Carol hoped that some of Sylvie's qualities would rub off on Felice, make her more relaxed and easier to be with.

Sylvie walked toward the others in the living room, but Felice tugged at Carol's arm and pulled her into the sitting room across the hall. Carol could hear Sylvie introducing herself. Yes, she would be able to get along on her own and establish a rapport with the other guests.

"I should be glad you've changed your mind about selling the house," Felice started immediately, without any preface, "but the circumstances are weird, Mother."

"Felice, I have guests waiting for me. I..."

"This can't wait. I'm worried about you. Who are these strangers living in your house? What do you know about them? Are you going to go out and leave them alone in the house? You have valuable furniture, antiques... they could rob you while you're gone....you know nothing about them."

"That's not true. I've explained this to you already, but you either didn't listen or forgot. I've been friends with Dottie for over a year now. She's visited me here and I've been to her house. I've met one of her sisters and her son. They are decent, honest people, and I'm in no danger of being robbed or murdered, if that's what you're worried about. They needed another place to live, and I needed someone to fill up this old house and keep me company."

"And where are they now? They should at least be doing the work, taking care of this party."

"They are friends, not servants," Carol protested. "And Dottie made all the wonderful hors d'oeuvres. Our agreement is that she and Margaret will help me take care of the house and pay some rent, but they are first and foremost friends. Dottie is at Margaret's high school dance this evening as a chaperone. You must come by sometime for dinner to meet them, when you are calmer."

"But how do you think it looks having strangers — renters — living here with you?"

"Why, I think it looks just fine. How fortunate I am to have found someone caring." Carol smiled happily. "Now, will you come into the living room? I think it's the height of rudeness for you to abandon Sylvie to strangers."

Carol turned and walked out of the sitting area and Felice followed. As they entered the living room, Josephine and Jack came in from the garden and greeted the newcomers. Carol made the necessary introductions.

Monique, Carol and Josephine stared in disbelief when Allison walked over to Maevis and gave her a hearty embrace. In return Maevis kissed Allison's cheek and said something about someone named Basil and his tomato plants. Then, seeing the astonishment on the others' faces, Maevis smiled and told them, "Oh, Allison and I had a long talk. We've reconciled. I'll give you the scoop later."

"Well," Carol sighed, "we're all here except Annie and her husband. When I saw her at the rink last week, she said they'd be here, didn't she, Maevis? You were there, too."

"Ahem," Maevis cleared her throat. "I have an important announcement to make on Annie's behalf. I'm supposed to inform everyone that she won't be coming today after all. She's on her way to... tah dah — drum roll, please — to Beijing!"

"Beijing?" they exclaimed in unison.

"What a surprise!"

"When did she decide this?"

"She phoned me just before she left yesterday," Maevis explained. "It was fairly sudden, though she's been wanting to go for awhile now. There was a last minute opening on one of the tours that her Chinese watercolor instructor leads and Annie took it. I'm so proud of her."

Allison was the first to recover from the news. "We all know she was searching for something new to do with her life. I hope she finds what she needs and returns to us soon safely."

"Yes," Carol added, "I've heard her talk about how much she loves Chinese art and culture."

"Anyone here been to China?" Brad asked them.

"I haven't," Earl answered, "but I know how to play chopsticks on the piano." He turned and plunked out a few notes.

"Oh, you found a doozy, Monique!" Maevis laughed, setting her celery stick down on a napkin. "I love him, and I know that song, too." She ran over and began poking at the keys of an upper octave while Earl played the bass notes of the duet.

"Go right ahead and enjoy yourselves everyone. I'll be in the kitchen." Carol smiled warmly. "But a little birdie told me that Brad is a wonderful baritone. I'd love to hear him."

"What would you like me to sing?" Brad asked, not needing to be prodded. "I know most of the old favorites."

"*My* hubby's got the words to all the standards stored in his brilliant noggin," Maevis bragged. "He loves to sing, but unfortunately he can't carry a tune."

"Well, I can probably play anything anyone wants to hear,"

Earl told them. The playing and singing began tentatively at first, then more confidently. *"I know a tear would glisten, if once more I could listen, to that gang that sang...."*

Carol came back into the parlor and harmonized, *"...heart of my heart.'* I haven't heard that one since the fifties. You two do have quite a repertoire, and Neal doesn't sound half bad. Would anyone like to see the rest of the house before dinner, now that we're all here?" she asked.

"If it's okay, Carol," Jack spoke up, "Josephine and I would like to go back outside again. We didn't get enough of your wonderful garden!"

"Of course, Jack," Carol answered as she placed her hand on the banister. She began to climb the wide curving staircase, followed by Monique, Allison and Maevis.

"C'mon, Sylvie, join us!" invited Carol.

<hr>

Josephine and Jack went out through the French doors again, Jack carrying their glasses of wine. Through the approaching dusk, Jo could still see the manicured hedges and masses of flowers. A row of lavender alongside a white lattice fence was fronted by pink English daisies. Toward the back of the yard, white roses clambered up a lattice archway. Beyond the arch was a winding stone path leading to a circle of roses — white, red and mottled. A line of eucalyptus trees enclosed the garden. The couple found an old glider nestled at the far end. Jack gave it a push.

"Let's sit here," he said to Josephine. "You can't find these old things much anymore. And not even a squeak! That lavender scent is very relaxing, too." He set their glasses down on a small table and helped Jo seat herself on the swing.

"I love that color combination. The purple against the white fence is so pleasing to look at," Jo commented, her eyes seeking out Jack's. "How peaceful it is here." She raised her chin towards him and their lips met. "This enchanting garden would be such a great spot for someone to get married in, don't you think, Jack?" she spoke quietly, finding his lips with her own once more.

"Do you mean us, Jo? You and me?"

Tears welled up in Josephine's eyes. Tiny, salty droplets rolled down her cheeks. Jack gently wiped them with his napkin.

"Yes, Jack. Oh, yes, my love. I'm ready now," Josephine whispered. "I know we can meet the future together, whatever it may bring."

"Josephine, I love you so much." Jack hugged her tightly.

"Do you think we might have our wedding here?" Jo asked when she'd recovered her voice. "It's absolutely perfect."

Jack's eyes lit up. "I'm sure Carol wouldn't object. I'll talk to her."

"I'm bursting with happiness, Jack. Let's go in and share the news."

"Yes, let's — in a minute." And then he kissed her again.

Inside, in the living room, the men had continued the piano playing and the robust singing, while Carol had taken her friends on the grand tour, climbing the polished mahogany steps. She stopped at the landing and said, "It's just the right time, late afternoon, to see the sun highlighting the colors of this stained glass window."

"Exquisite! And it's such an unusual shape," Allison murmured.

"Yes, an octagon," Carol added.

"I love the blue of the stream running through the meadow." Sylvie moved a step closer to the window to take a better look.

After many *oohs* and *aahs* of admiration at the parqueted hall flooring upstairs and an old secretary desk that Carol obviously still used, they collapsed on a deep blue velvet sofa in the second-floor sitting room. Two club chairs matched the sofa. "This isn't a fainting couch, is it?" Maevis joked.

"How long did you say you've lived here, Carol?" asked Allison.

"I've been in this house for over thirty years. Robert and I bought it after a particularly successful year, and I have been collecting antiques for almost as long. And now Dottie and Margaret will be enjoying all this beauty with me, and helping me to maintain it. Maybe I'll eventually bequeath the house to the city for a good cause, who knows? It's mine to do with as I wish. I certainly don't need anyone's permission."

Maevis looked at Carol in admiration. "Boy, you've certainly changed a lot, Carol, and for the better, I might add. Not that I didn't love you to bits before," she added hurriedly.

"Speaking of changes, and people living together and such, guess who's coming to live with me at my place?" Monique's eyes gleamed. "Earl, of course. We love each other, and we want to grab whatever happiness we can."

"Monique, you didn't tell me!" Carol exclaimed.

"We won't marry. I admit I'm a little embarrassed to be living with a man without the marriage ceremony, but we're going to do it anyway."

"Good for you, Monique. I think Earl's a real sweetheart. By the way," Maevis volunteered. "Allison and I have made up, and... oh, we've all so much to be thankful for." She stopped to take a breath. "Listen, I want everyone to come to my humble abode next time for a big barbeque — with kids, hot dogs and hamburgers — vegetarian, naturally — and lots of other culinary delicacies. Whattaya say?"

"That sounds wonderful, Maevis," Allison accepted. "And while we're here, let me thank you all once more. You saved my life, you know, in more ways than one. Not only what Annie did, but everything. Your visits, your concern, your advice and — well, your perfect friendship.

"I've worked out a lot of things in my life. I've washed Alex out of my hair, taken Brad back into my heart, and I have some other exciting news too. For the past month I have been interviewing for the position of director of the Bay Area Council for Children. A few days ago the deal was cemented, and I waited to tell all of you when we were together. Not only am I to be responsible for the management and operation of the BACC, I will also be representing and promoting the agency at the state and national level.

"I went back and visited my second graders before the year was over, and I know I'm going to miss them a lot, but I'm really looking forward to this new challenge. I'm a lucky lady, and I thank all of you for...for...well, you know what for," Allison concluded.

They heard the French doors opening. Allison peeked over the banister. "Oh, here come Jo and Jack," she announced. "Let's go downstairs, shall we?"

Josephine was leaning on Jack's arm, flushed and smiling a most beautiful smile.

"Listen up, everyone," she called out.

The piano-playing and singing stopped and everyone turned towards them. Looking directly at her very good friends, Josephine asked in a clear, but dreamy voice, "Who wants to be a bridesmaid?"

Everybody started talking at once.

"I knew it," yelled Maevis to no one in particular.

"I'm so happy for you both," Monique called out.

The men shook Jack's hand and slapped him on the back. "Way to go!" said Neal, as Earl and Brad followed with congratulations.

Allison waded into the middle of the group and hugged her best friend. Carol was next in line. "I think it was the effect of my garden," she said, "They were out there long enough."

"No, it wasn't. It was our crooning," Earl countered.

"And," Carol continued, proclaiming, "I think my garden is just the place to get married, don't you, Jo?"

"Yes. Yes, I do."

Authors

H. Reese *is the pseudonym of 6 women:* ***H****elen Leon Gendler,* ***R****osa Zaks Feldman,* ***E****die Kulstein,* ***E****laine Kahn,* ***S****andy Paller,* *and a silent* ***E****.*